DIANESHERRYCASE

elephant
milk

Miraculous Books

Miraculous Books

ISBN: 978-0-615-38094-0

PRINTED IN THE UNITED STATES OF AMERICA

For
Leah Case and Natalie Case

1

Beverly Hills, California, August 1969

I HAD JUST TURNED 17, and I was driving a lime green dune buggy that used to belong to Elvis. A movie was about to be released with my accidentally naked breasts in it, and I had just watched my best girlfriend shoot heroin while Keith Richards nodded on the couch. I parked on Coldwater Canyon, walked down the hill, and lit a joint to calm down. There, I found a pile of black clothes, wet with blood. The Tate murders? It was 1969 and things were starting to get icky.

I got home after finding those bloody clothes and my mom was gone, with a note saying that she'd be in the desert for a few days. I needed something to eat or drink or do, but nothing sounded good or filling or possible. My skin was closing in on me. I wanted to scream or hit someone. No one was home.

I put water in a pan, determined to think of nothing else, just stare at the water until it boiled. Steam formed quickly in my head, telling me how scary life was, how I was missing information, missing being held, missing something. I tried to concentrate on the water, but all I could think about was Frank and how warm I had felt when he was near.

My face burned from the steam. I thought about Jack and how I never told Mom he touched me, because she probably wouldn't have believed me anyway and she was happy with him, for better or for worse, whatever that meant. The water moved, but didn't boil. Oh God, what the hell was I supposed to do about that movie. It would break my Grandma's Baptist heart if she ever knew I posed half-naked.

I kept thinking about all this and my mind got more and more confused like a photo in developing chemicals except reversed, from the crisp image back to the grey smear. The only clear vision was that dreamy goodnight kiss and the postcard from Mazatlán with my two favorite words: Love, Frank.

The water broke into a big boil right before my eyes.

2

Venice Beach, April 1969

I FIRST MET FRANK ON Venice Beach, where I wasn't allowed to go and when I should have been in school. A psychedelic Hindu god and goddess made love on a purple cloud in a painting on the cinderblock wall. Sweet-smelling smoke drifted through the beaded door of the head shop.

Hippies, a few years older than us, wore long dresses and Indian scarves. Old guys with beards gathered on park benches, drank out of jugs or paper bags and looked less like footloose travelers, more like bums. There were runaways too, kids my age, tanned and dirty with backpacks and fringe jackets.

My girlfriend Julia and I had hitched a ride with our English teacher, Kenny. He liked Julia because he said she was a cross be-tween Bridget Bardot and Janis Joplin. We all planned to spend the afternoon wandering around Venice, but Julia disappeared into Kenny's second-floor apartment when he offered her some pot. I hung out by myself on the boardwalk. Until this short-haired military-looking man started bothering me.

"Hey beautiful, let's you and me, what do you say?"

I walked away. The sky was gray and the trashcans were overflowing. I heard music. It sounded like some old black guy singing the blues. A group of people had gathered on the beach. I walked over there and inched my way into the crowd.

A white kid stood in the sand, singing and playing his guitar. He was a few years older than me -- maybe twenty. He wore jeans and a dirty suede jacket, even though it wasn't cold. His face hid behind his long dark hair, but when I finally saw it, I saw whiskers soft enough to touch. I saw strong high cheekbones and dark deep-set eyes.

A gray, faded Stetson was upside down on the ground in front of him and occasionally someone tossed in a coin. The military guy tossed a penny in and laughed. Then he tried to put his arm around me. "Be my girl, man," he yelled, oblivious to the music.

The musician walked straight up to the military guy and sang furiously loud, right in his face. It was so powerful that the military guy disappeared. Then he continued singing, in a soft voice now. The song was about night skies and the moon reflecting in warm muddy water. The musician looked at me for just a moment. He quickly looked back down, his shoulders curved around the guitar. I could feel that my presence had changed him. He would know, without looking up, if I left.

His hands were fast and sure as he fingered the strings of his guitar. I had never really noticed how close the shape of a guitar is to the shape of a woman's body.

When the song was finished, people threw quarters and dropped dollar bills into his hat. He stood up, mumbled thanks, and stuffed the money into his jeans' pocket.

The crowd had dispersed and I felt silly standing there. There was a spot on the toe of my right boot. I licked my finger and tried to wipe it off.

"Cool boots," he said. "They new?"

"Yeah." I was glad I'd worn them. "That was a good song," I said, still looking down. "I never heard it before."

"I made it up."

"Really, you wrote it? It was beautiful." I looked at him and my breath felt weak. I had a powerful urge to run, but his eyes wouldn't let mine go. They were the color of warm earth, half-closed and gently focused, with a longing I understood.

"Did you ever feel like there was something so wrong with the world, that if you looked behind you fast enough, you'd find the mistake? Like maybe they forgot to fill in all the colors?" His voice was as deep and soothing as the rumble of a secret.

"I know what you mean," I said. "Sometimes I feel like my back is naked and I only have clothes on in front."

"Did you take acid, too?"

"Yeah. Nine times. Freaked me out."

"Me, too. I don't think it's such a great idea."

He played a few chords and sighed like a tired old soul determined to plug on. "Those boots will get good in a few years," he said. "You gotta rough 'em up. Kick stuff. Wear 'em a lot. Don't be careful."

It began to sprinkle. Frank played a Stones song, with a long whiny harmonica solo. "…Thank you for your wine, California. Thank you for your sweet and bitter…" His low voice hit deep inside my body.

I watched raindrops fall on his face like tears streaming down. He pulled the bottom of his coat up over his head as the rain got stronger. He hunched over his guitar to shelter it, played a few more licks, then stopped and looked out from under his coat-tent. His lips were wet. They wanted to be kissed.

"Okay," he said. "Want to go?"

"Yes," I said. I was nearly seventeen. Way too old to be a virgin.

It was an old blue anonymous car, like a plainclothes police car except it was a convertible.

"I'm Sean," I said, as he cleaned off the front seat for me.

"Frank."

Frank spread a towel out over the torn seat on the passenger side. He tossed some trash and magazines and a yellow pad into the back seat, which was already crowded with blankets, clothes, a box of books, and a wadded-up orange tarp.

Frank got in and started the car, drove several blocks, then parked in an alley behind an Italian restaurant.

"I ordered a pizza," he said. "About an hour ago. It ought to end up in that trash any minute now."

He'd ordered it from a phone booth to an address close by, knowing that when the pizza was delivered, whoever lived there would tell the delivery boy they hadn't ordered it. It was a complicated pizza: pineapple, mushrooms and sausage. One they couldn't sell easily.

So it ended up in the garbage behind the restaurant. We found it, still hot in the box. Frank was a genius at getting by. Never once called home. I wanted to marry him.

Rain hit the canvas top in little thuds that almost tickled. Water poured down onto my right arm from where the door closed. Frank and I stared at each other, listening together. It felt like we were touching, but we weren't.

"That's real music," he said. "Look at the windshield."

Tiny crystal raindrops formed on the glass and rolled down like slow mercury. One grew large and gathered momentum until it slid down the windshield, picking up others in its track. Frank saw music everywhere.

He pulled the armrest up from between us. It was an old-fashioned front seat, like a couch. He sat beside me, his face only a few inches from mine. He smelled warm and dusty.

"The blue in your eyes is so clear in this light," he said, "it's almost transparent."

"Don't say that," I answered, slightly panicked. It looked solid and safe behind his dark eyes. If I could only get back there with him, I might be safe too.

Frank leaned over to the back seat and grabbed the orange tarp. "Check this out."

He got out and covered the car with the tarp, crawling under it to get back in. It was dark in the car.

"I sleep here. No one bothers me," Frank said. "Welcome to my home."

It felt like we were children in a blanket tent.

He turned my body towards his and pulled me so close that I felt his chest rise and fall against my breasts. He rubbed his cheek slowly against my face. The window fogged as we breathed together, in and out. His whiskers felt slightly mean.

Frank lay down on the seat and pulled me on top of him. For a moment, I tried to push away. But when my lower body touched his, the warmth burned through my clothing and I melted onto him. Our bodies took on a life of their own.

We writhed and stroked and rubbed and touched as much of each other as we possibly could. Then we took off our pants and slowed down.

It was just skin at first. It seemed like hours full of minutes of soft, soft skin, and as we got closer and closer, I was afraid. But he was so oddly there, so sweet and strong.

With the eager glee of a child, he filled me. So hearty was his hunger that it hurt deep inside, but I didn't mind at all. Frank was making me a woman.

I sat there, half-naked, my head still reeling. Frank was already dressed, keys in hand.

I pulled my pants back on. Frank got out and took the tarp off. The sun had come out, but was setting.

I took a deep breath.

"Aren't you ever going to kiss me?" I said.

He started the car and gunned off like he was being chased by a cop.

"It's all fucked up," he said. "You can't bring kids into a world like this."

"Who said anything about kids?"

"It's powerful stuff, sex. Making love makes people. This world forgot that. It's all fucked up."

I finished zipping my jeans and threw the towel we had been lying on, with a small spot of my blood on it, into the back seat.

"There are some good things in the world," I said.

"Sure," he said. "But if it weren't for rock and roll, this whole century would be a bust."

3

Songs That Felt Like Love

MY MOTHER WAS ASLEEP WHEN I got home and I was hungry. I fixed myself some Frosted Flakes and then realized the milk was sour.

"What time is it?" Mom asked when she came in. She poured herself a gin and tonic while the coffee heated.

"About four," I guessed. The clock above the sink had been broken since way before she kicked my father out, and I don't think the one on the stove was ever meant to work at all. Besides that, all the numbers were scrubbed off the temperature knob so you never knew how hot the oven was.

"Alex didn't call?"

"Nobody called. Except Dad." He had actually called two days before but I forgot to tell her.

"What did he want?"

I ate an Oreo and smelled the milk again. Yep, it was bad.

"What did your father want?"

"He wanted to know if I was going to see him Sunday."

"Is that all he said?" She poured herself some coffee, added sour milk, and took a sip. "Oh shit." She slammed the cup down. "Why didn't anybody throw this out?"

The phone rang and Mom dashed for it quicker than I could. I knew it was Alex by the sweetie-pie voice she used. "Oh great, what time?" She had this little girl smile on her face and she was wiggling her toes.

When she got off the phone she started scurrying around, picking up newspapers and emptying ashtrays with old Kleenex in them. "Honey, do me a big favor." She handed me ten bucks. "One of those barbecued chickens and some lettuce and uhm, tomatoes. And cigarettes."

She was in a great mood when I got back from the market. We set the table with bright yellow place mats and joked about how hot it was, trying to top each other with "it's hotter than...."

"It's hotter than a blistered pussy in a pepper patch," she said and we both laughed so hard we almost wet our pants. Then Alex arrived in his cop uniform, and Mom told me I was too young to wear lipstick and that I should go put on a bra.

Alex was looking very grim and he had sweat on his hairy neck. Mom gave him a big hug, and he grabbed her ass and lifted her so that her bare feet were barely touching the carpet. Then he finally said hello to me. We never really talked much. He had only been around a few weeks, and most of that time he was busy doing it with Mom. I don't think they ever talked much either. But they couldn't keep their hands off each other.

That night they went more or less straight to the bedroom. Only instead of the usual bedsprings, I heard them fighting. "Just give me time," he screamed.

I finished my dinner and went to my room. I turned off the lights and got under the covers and made up a story about Frank and me.

Frank stroked my cheek and said, "God, you're pretty. Prettiest girl I've ever seen."

Then he grabbed me by both arms and threw me down onto a patch of cactus with red succulent flowers that smelled like peaches. He did a savage dance as if he were a cannibal around a campfire. He screamed and sang like a madman, and ripped off my clothes, swearing he would devour me. He licked my body until I was excited beyond fear or pain.

And I surrendered fully, into the prickly piercing cactus.

It's a good thing all Mom modeled was hands because her face looked worn out, as if she'd been up all night. She sat at the dining table painting her nails, getting ready for her first job in a long time. Alex was in his cop uniform, staring at the television, reclining on the couch. The silence between them was deadly. Alex switched the channel.

"I wanted to watch that," my mother said. Alex kept changing the channels.

"I said I wanted to watch that!"

"What the hell's the matter with you?" Alex yelled. He stood up and grabbed his cop hat. "Jesus Christ, Eudora! This is getting worse than home."

Alex stomped toward the front door, and Mom followed, whining, "Don't leave."

"I'm sick of this shit," he shouted. He slammed out.

A few minutes later, my mother came into the kitchen with one hand up over her shoulder. I thought she was going to hit me.

"Why are you flinching, Sean? Jesus. No one's going to hit you. You haven't done anything." She looked at me, suddenly curious. "Have you?"

"I don't know. Why do you have your hand up like that?"

"I'm practicing. I'm doing a television commercial tomorrow. See. You hold your hand like this for a few minutes, and then when you go to film, the veins won't stick out. It only lasts a few moments, but it works. My agent taught me. She used to be an actress, too."

Whenever Eudora was angry with Alex she would dress herself all gorgeous and pick me up from my part-time job so she could flirt with my boss. Jack was fifty-ish and had two grown sons. We'd met him when Mom was on her clothes-buying binge after her first fight with Alex. I went with her to every store within fifty miles trying to help her feel better, until we finally had to tear up all the credit cards.

Jumping Jax was the sort of store that rock stars shopped in. It had every kind of cowboy boot imaginable, lots of black stretchy pants, dresses that showed everything and shirts made of leather and lace.

Mom thought Jack was good-looking, but once men had bald spots I could never call them good-looking. He wore his shirt half-unbuttoned, which was surprising given that he had good taste in clothes. The hair on his chest was gray and there was a scar up the middle as if someone had opened him up to store ice.

For a while, Mom just flirted with Jack when she was mad at Alex. Then Alex would call, and she wouldn't talk to Jack again until she got into another fight with Alex. That made Jack like her even more and he'd send her presents, clothes from the store and flowers. "Aren't older men terrific?" she would say.

Jack gave me the job even though I was young and inexperienced. He spent time teaching me about fashion and what makes a woman look good, and he gave me rides home in his antique Rolls. "So, you like working for me?"

I told him yeah, I liked it, and he told me I was doing a good job. That felt great.

So did making money, for the apartment I would get the second

I turned eighteen. But my savings plan wasn't working out. The first time I got a paycheck I used the whole thing to buy cowboy boots. Now I had to buy a hat.

After work on Saturday, I put on my boots and took the bus to Venice.

I found Frank right away, sitting on his bench, like he was waiting for me. He had a yellow pad on his lap and a bunch of harmonicas beside him. He didn't say anything, but he cleared off a place for me to sit.

He scribbled some words on his pad and then, as if to himself, he read what he had written. "It rained, I touched stone faces." He paused and stared at me, as though looking for something.

"How about this," he said. "'White tears flowed from her eyes.'"

"Cool." I noticed a tattoo on his shoulder, a girl's name. "Who's Eva?"

"I don't want to talk about it. I'm writing." Frank studied his yellow pad for a moment. "I can't finish this damned song. Shit." He ripped the page off and crumpled it.

"No big deal. You'll finish later."

We watched a Mexican couple cooking lunch on a small hibachi. They had about a dozen children around them. Some were helping, the smallest was hanging on his mother's leg. A couple were fighting, the others played with a small football.

"I'm not your boyfriend," Frank said.

"I know. We just met." The football came at us and Frank caught it and tossed it
back.

"My mom has five brothers back in Tennessee. I wish I had a brother or sister," I said.

"Me too. I used to have a cat." Frank laughed, deep in his throat. His eyes followed a slow moving cloud.

"My mother used to watch me practice piano," he said in a voice lower than his normal speaking voice. "She'd stand over me, breathing down my neck. Once, my cat jumped onto the piano bench and suddenly pounced up into her face and grabbed onto her. He stuck his nails into the collar of her dress, and just hung there. Mom screamed and ran out of the room, pulling at the cat, trying to get him off. I didn't help her. I just kept on playing."

"'I think he willed it,' she told my dad. 'He just kept on playing, like he was hypnotized or something.' I didn't hear my dad's answer, but from then on, my father flew off the handle at any little thing. He'd say 'Why are you staring at me like that?' and I'd say, 'I'm staring at you?' and he would haul off and hit me.

"Then one day he drove away and never came back. Drove off a cliff on purpose. I never knew who drove who to what."

Frank's laugh was just two notes long, more a groan than real laughter. I felt so sorry for him, I just wanted to take him in my arms.

He got up and grabbed his guitar. "Got an errand. Wanna come?"

"I'm glad you kept playing, Frank."

He thought about it for a moment and shrugged. "I was in the middle of a song."

We walked to the tattoo parlor on Rose. We looked at the drawings in the window and Frank finally chose a picture of a big red koi fish.

"Who's Eva?" I asked.

"Doesn't matter. This koi will cover her right up."

We went inside and he settled into the barber chair. A huge Harley kind of guy smeared Frank's arm with alcohol. The guy stuck a needle right into the E and started drawing the tattoo. Frank ignored him.

"Those boots will get good. Just wait."

"Yeah, they're still kind of new." I watched as drops of blood gathered around Eva. "But they hurt my feet."

"Too tight?" Frank asked, acting like nothing was bothering him.

"Just the left one. Just a little."

"Put water on it. When you wear 'em. They'll stretch." Frank's lips tightened just a wee bit and he didn't talk for a second. "Spray 'em. They'll fit good. Water's the way."

The tattoo took forever. It looked like it hurt, but Frank pretended it was nothing. The big guy put a bandage on it and we got up to leave.

"Okay, that's twenty bucks," the leather guy said. "They like those koi in Japan. Know why?"

"Why?" Frank asked, pulling out his wallet.

"They're the only kind of fish that doesn't flop around when you go to cut its head off."

Frank gave him the money. "Yeah, right," he said, like he already knew that.

The sun was going down and I didn't care that I was late getting home. We sat in the sand and Frank played guitar with his eyes closed. It was a Mexican song, the kind that makes you want to cry before the lyrics even start.

His hair fell over his face as he played this same song, over and over, until it got dark, and we lay on our backs and stared at the sky.

The sky was a deep dark blue and Frank talked about this huge eclipse that was going to happen on his twenty-first birthday, nine months from now. He said it would be most visible in the mountains of Chiapas. He said he'd rather die than miss it.

"Where is Chiapas?"

"Southern Mexico. But I'm going to the beach first. Mazatlán. Warm water. Good waves."

There was something I wanted to ask for, again, but I was afraid he'd think it was silly. I took a deep breath and asked anyway. I had to.

"Aren't we ever going to kiss?" I said. I didn't touch him, I just asked.

"I told you before. No more sex. It would be awful."

"Awful?"

"We'd both be miserable, sooner or later." Frank reached in the back and grabbed his old Stetson.

"Didn't you like it?"

"Yeah, sure, that's not the point. You're too young to understand, Sean. I made a mistake. You want a ride home?"

Eudora was crying in her bedroom when I got back. I tried to ignore it and keep the smile I had left from Frank, but her sobs seemed to get louder and crawl into my head.

I found her in bed, her arms wrapped around a wet pillow with eye makeup all over it. I asked what the matter was.

"I just can't stand it anymore," she said. "I just can't stand it." I stroked her head like she used to do when I was little. That seemed to make her cry more.

"Look at this," she said, showing me a picture in the local paper. "Just look at that." It was an awards ceremony for cops and Alex was there with his policewoman wife, looking perfectly happy and posing with the mayor. "I feel like a goddamned fool."

I wanted to tell her she was one. But I hated to see my momma cry. I brought her dinner in bed that night. She loved to have someone take care of her.

"You're not mad at me?" she said. She reminded me of a sixth grader who used to have a crush on me.

"No, I'm not mad," I told her.

"I can't get used to sleeping alone," Mom said putting her head down on my lap. "Your father and I got married when I wasn't much older than you."

I knew that and I also knew that she didn't get to go to her senior prom because she was pregnant with me and had to drop out. And that Dad had to walk forever to school in the snow and that I'd had it real good.

I made her a drink and lay down with her until she fell asleep.

Jack sent my mother tons of presents, and she made me answer the phone all the time and tell him she was out. "I thought you wanted someone rich and single," I'd tell her.

"Love is more important," she'd say and wait for Alex to call.

Jack was used to getting what he wanted and he was getting pissed. Finally he stopped sending her presents and started calling her a bitch, as in, "How's that bitch you live with?"

"Fine," I'd tell him.

Jack called me up to his office after all the other salesgirls had gone home. I didn't know if he was going to fire me or give me a raise.

"Your red hair is so beautiful," he said. His held a strand of my long hair, and let his fingers linger on my breast a moment, before tossing the hair over my shoulder. "But don't let it cover those."

He pulled down the shoulder of my tank top. "Don't pull away, I'm just admiring your breasts. So pretty."

"Look, I have to go to my boyfriend's," I lied.

"Just let me look a minute. Just one minute. Please."

I didn't know what to do. I felt like I was going to throw up. But I didn't want to cause a scene and I didn't want to lose my job and he did keep it under a minute.

Frank disappeared. I went to the beach about fifty times, hoping to run into him. I walked and walked, and when that didn't work, I hung out on his bench, pretending to write. The sun on my face was hot and I wished my white skin were thicker. If I just stayed on his bench long enough, he was bound to come. So I looked down at my paper, and drew. Every time I'd hear footsteps, I'd try to act cool and casual and not look at the face right off, knowing I'd recognize him

17

from the waist down. But I didn't see him that whole week. Hundreds of legs passed, but not one of them was Frank's.

I shopped endlessly until I found a hat. Julia and I looked up and down Beverly Drive and then we hitchhiked into Hollywood. We finally found my hat at a little shop called Granny's on the Strip. It was royal blue flannel, big and floppy. I tied a beautiful paisley scarf around it and Julia stuck in a white feather she had found on the beach. The hat was perfectly me.

Every night I stayed home, thinking maybe he would call. I wore my hat so it would get more soulful, and I sprayed my cowboy boots with water every day. They were starting to feel better. Frank knew so much.

Mom finally pulled herself together and called Jack. He sent her two-dozen roses and a crystal perfume sprayer. Mom bought a bunch of new make-up and pastel towels with matching sheets for her bed. They made a date.

The first time Jack came to our door Mom was doing her nails. She had developed a thing about hands. She was even starting to like statues of Jesus' hands and she was never that crazy about Jesus himself.

"You inherited perfect hands," she told me.

"That'll be handy," I said, pouring myself a bowl of Frosted Flakes with my great hands.

"Don't knock it," she said. "You inherited lots of fabulous qualities from your old mom. Look at those cheekbones."

She raised her face so the fluorescent light could compliment her perfect cheekbones. "Comes from Indian blood."

"What Indian blood?" I asked.

"Oh, I don't know," she said, distracted by the doorbell. "That's Jack. Answer it, will you?"

"I'm busy," I said, making a beeline to my room.

I didn't tell her why I hated him. I figured she would just blame me if I told her. I also didn't want to ruin her big chance. She was thirty-three and losing her looks.

But she was pissed that I wouldn't answer the door or say hello to Jack. "You little bitch," she said, smacking her new orange lipstick.

When they left that day, I poured the perfume out of the bottle Jack had bought her and replaced it with bug spray.

Frank had just started his car when I saw him. I ran to catch him before he pulled away. I yanked opened the passenger door and just stood there in the engine noise.

"Nice hat," Frank finally said. "Is that new?"

Frank turned off the engine. I wanted to touch him and scream *Take me in your arms forever, kiss me, hold me, please.*

"It's my birthday," I said, quickly.

"Seventeen?"

"How did you know?"

"I got to go. You coming?"

We pulled into a shopping center and Frank made me wait in the car. He came out carrying a birthday cake. He put the top down on the car and drove up to Mulholland.

Frank spread out an old wool blanket. We sat on it and ate cake with our hands. My hair was all blown free and my smile was close to bursting.

"Check this out," he said, getting chocolate on his passport. "You should get one of these. Never know when you might want to go somewhere."

Frank told me about places in Mexico where monkeys cry in the night and thick jungle grows so fast you can watch it grow and the ancient secrets of man are written on pyramid walls. Listening to him took me away.

"Where I'm going there are stars in the sky and music as old as the earth itself. All I take is my guitar. I'll be swimming in warm water. Won't be back for a while."

"Why not?" I asked. I'd gotten this idea and I casually unbuttoned my denim blouse.

Frank put his passport in his hip pocket.

"There are stars in the sky here, too," I said, shaking as I opened my shirt. "You just can't see them."

I wasn't wearing a bra. My breasts were naked in the evening air. Frank looked carefully, like he was in awe. Like my breasts were holy objects.

"Do you want to kiss them?" I said.

"I just want to look."

Frank gently placed my shoulders back, so that I sat up straight.

With two fingers, he lightly circled each nipple, until they felt like they might burst.

I reached out to him, but he took my hands in his and kissed them. Then he buttoned my blouse and picked up his guitar.

"Don't you want to make love?" I said.

Frank smiled, enjoying teasing me. "We just did."

"But, Frank..."

His face turned serious. "Not on your birthday," he said. "Not when I'm leaving."

There was no doubt in my mind that he loved me.

"Adios," Frank said, when we pulled up a block from my house.

"See you tomorrow?"

"I'm history," he said.

"You're leaving?"

Frank nodded.

"Now?"

"Late. Midnight flight."

"When will I see you?"

"You're seeing me now." Frank's face broke into a big smile. "Leaving for the airport at ten. You coming? We'll meet you down the block."

The house was ridiculously clean when I got home. There was a framed photo on the coffee table that I hadn't seen in a long time. It was a picture of the three of us, years ago. In it, Mom is a fat-faced teenage girl with bright red lipstick, who had eloped nine months before with her sailor. My father holds their new little baby girl and grins. His Pall Malls are stuck up the sleeve of a white T-shirt.

"Your father's coming at eight for dinner," Mom told me. I must have given her some kind of look, but I didn't say a word. "What's wrong with that? Your father and I happen to be old friends. I've known him longer than I've known anybody."

"I thought he was boring," I said, quoting her. "I thought he worked too hard and wouldn't buy a house with a pool anyway."

Mom squinted and glared at me. "You don't know anything," she said.

"Fine," was all I could think of to say.

Dad came and knocked on the door. I think that made all of us feel really weird. He'd lived there for six years and now he was knocking on the door like a stranger.

"What's the matter with you, aren't you going to answer it?" Mom yelled. She was in the bathroom primping just like she did when Jack was expected. Putting bug spray under her ears no doubt.

I opened the door and Dad just stood there, awkwardly. He had flowers in one hand and a brown paper bag in the other.

"Happy birthday." He handed me two jars of gooseberry jam that Grandpa had sent back with him and a birthday present. I put the jam in the kitchen while Dad came in and stood around looking out of place in the living room.

After a short time Mom breezed out of the bathroom like somebody joining a mid-summer dance. She seemed a bit knocked off balance the second she saw him, though, and they both stood there in shock for a moment. And then Dad handed her the flowers. "The place looks neater than it ever did," he said, meaning 'great, I leave and now you start cleaning house.'

Mom got it. "Flowers for me?" she said. "That's a first." Dad cracked his knuckles.

It was those same two who used to sit on my bed while she sang "Goodnight Sweetheart, well it's time to go," and he did a funny baritone doo-doo-doot, doot, doo-doo.

"I'm going to Julia's." I started toward the door.

"You're not going anywhere," Mom said.

"What's the matter with you?" Dad asked. Just like when we all lived together.

I tried to sit still for dinner. Dad talked about his work and how it was coming upon the busy season, and Mom talked about her new rich boyfriend and how we should all have Thanksgiving together.

I didn't say a word until 9:55 when I excused myself to go to the bathroom. I grabbed my hat, climbed out my bedroom window and ran down the street.

Bidlo drove because Frank sold him the car. Bidlo had freckles and his eyes never stood still, not even for a moment.

Frank sat alone in back, drumming his knees to the music on the radio.

"Have you guys known each other long?" I asked Bidlo.

"Nobody knows Frank long. He's a rare one," said Bidlo. He had a southern accent and bit hard on the toothpick in his mouth as his eyes darted around.

I laughed for no reason whatsoever. "Too bad he's leaving."

"A guy like that is good to know. Even if he is gone."

Bidlo pulled up to the curb. A loud recording told us that the area was for loading and unloading only. Frank jumped out and said, "Thanks for the ride."

I suddenly had the feeling he was never coming back.

"Bye, Sean," he said. "I'll send you a card from Mazatlán."

My nose tickled so badly it hurt, and I tried to hide my eyes. Frank put his hand on my head and turned my face toward his.

"Cool hat," he said. A large tear fell off my cheek. "But you gotta rough it up a little. Give it some soul."

I could barely talk. "How?"

"I don't know. Run over it with a truck."

"I don't have a truck, Frank."

"Here. Let me have it." Frank grabbed my hat, threw it on the ground and stomped on it with his boot a few times. Then he brushed it off and put it back on my head. "There you go." I had to laugh. "Isn't that better?" he asked.

"Do you love me, Frank?" I asked, in spite of the part of me that still wanted to be cool.

A cop pulled up and tried to wave us on, out of the white zone. Frank smoothed my hair off my face, and tucked it behind my ears.

"Don't worry," he said. "You are loved."

He lifted my face towards his. Then he kissed me deep. Like I had always wanted.

Frank waved over his shoulder. I watched him disappear through the automatic door.

4

The Comforted

"WOMEN ARE MORE IMPORTANT TO Jewish men," Mom said. "Jack listens to my advice." Mom had dragged me to lunch at the Bel Air Hotel so she could tell me some 'important news'.

A bee settled on my Hawaiian papaya and seafood salad.

"You listen to me, Sean. It's just as easy to fall in love with someone rich. That's why I'm smart this time."

The bee flew into Mom's face. She jumped up, screamed and slapped the air in front of her. Everyone looked at us. Mom wore a tight purple skirt with high heels.

"Can't you get rid of these bees?" she yelled at a passing waiter.

He set his tray down and started swatting. "So sorry, ma'am."

"I just can't believe I'm paying twenty-five dollars for lunch and I still have to put up with insects."

"If you like, ma'am, I can move you to another table."

Mom grabbed her purse and headed toward the table with the reserved sign on it, the table she had wanted in the first place. The waiter scooted after her, carrying her wine glass and shrimp cocktail. I followed with my Hawaiian salad and iced tea.

"Sean!" my mother said when we'd arrived at the table. Whispered shouts were her specialty. "Haven't I taught you anything? God." She sat down, looked embarrassed, and spoke in a low, forceful voice. "A lady never, ever, carries her drink across a restaurant. Do you hear me?"

A busboy filled our glasses with water. Mom tossed a sweet open smile at a dark-eyed man at the next table.

"I have to go to the bathroom," I said. I grabbed my purse and walked quickly past the man Mom had smiled at.

"Excuse me, miss," he said softly, as if any word from him could stop me.

"You're excused." I kept walking.

He grabbed my arm. "Wait a minute." He had a French accent and held his cigarette close to his mouth when he spoke. "This gentleman and I have a bet on your age."

"How much?"

The other man laughed. I pegged him as a rich producer because he was chubby and old, and his arm was around a beautiful blonde.

"You don't have a clue who you're talking to," he said. "Do you? Don Richard has made more stars than God."

"I still have to go to the bathroom."

I stayed in the bathroom as long as I could, looking in the mirror to see if I really looked seventeen. I brushed my long red hair over my yellow tube top, trying to cover my breasts.

When I returned to the patio, the guy with the cigarette was sitting in my seat and Mom was laughing with her head thrown back. The way she laughed like that, with a wide-open mouth, was what made men fall in love with her. At least that's what she'd told me.

"Is this your sister?" the guy asked Mom as I came up to the table.

"You flatter me," she said in a brand new breathy European accent. She smiled lovingly at me and stroked my hair. "She's beautiful, isn't she?" Her lips pursed as she spoke.

The man laughed. He took Mom's hand in his and kissed it. "You must be actresses, both of you," he purred. "Both so beautiful."

"Of course we are." Mom smiled grandly, an almost English accent this time, quite theatrical.

"Mom?" I said, still standing over them. "What happened to my salad?"

"Oh darling, I thought you were finished."

The guy got up and slipped our check into the palm of his hand, leaving a business card in its place. He slid an upside down crystal wine glass from the center of the table to the empty spot in front of my seat. Then he kissed Mom's hand again. "I'm delighted," he said.

Mom's face looked up at him with a frozen smile and watched as he left the room. In front of me, under the upturned glass, the bee he'd caught buzzed around, bumping its head against the crystal.

Jack was in one of his domestic moods, cooking chicken, when the script came. "THE COMFORTED" was written in big bold letters and a note paper clipped to the red cardboard cover said, "for the role of Veronica."

I was at the dining table trying to fill out an application to Berkeley. Not that I really planned to go to college. I'd sat in schools eleven years already and still hadn't learned how to keep my man.

"Men aren't everything," Julia had said. "Throw yourself into something."

"A boiling vat?"

"There's always drugs," she said. But I didn't have any. So I filled out college applications.

Question: 'Describe your goals in 250 words.'

Answer: 'To get the hell out of this kitchen.' (That's only eight words.)

"They called my old agent," Mom lied to Jack while she poured herself a glass of wine. She had promised Jack she wasn't going to act anymore, but it was only because she'd never gotten a job anyway. Just those hand inserts.

"This oven isn't heating up," Jack yelled. "What's the matter with the damned thing?"

"Beats me," said Mom. She came back into the dining room and sat down beside me with her script. "It stars Dick Rand." And then she whispered. "Remember, Sean? That was him, in case you didn't know, sitting with Don Richard." She started thumbing through the script.

"This chicken's still frozen, can I cook it frozen?" Jack dropped a pan on the kitchen floor.

"They need to know my major and my career objectives," I said. "I want to study women and religion and anthropology and animal psychology. I don't know how to make that into a career."

Mom didn't hear me. She was flipping through the script, looking for her character. "There's a good part here for the shrink's wife, but that's not Veronica."

"What temperature do I cook this at?" Jack said.

"Objective, colon." I printed in felt tip. "To be a feminologist, comparing females in the animal kingdom and women of various cultures. Or better yet, a masculinologist, specializing in street males of Anglo descent in Latin America. Think I could get a grant?"

"Here it is - Veronica, red hair and a cute little figure."

Mom took a sip of her wine and kept reading. "Veronica is mysteriously flirtatious, intelligent, and a very sweet sixteen...."

"Where's a spatula?" Jack asked, poking his head through the kitchen door.

Mom threw the script down on the dining table, spilling her wine all over my application. "You've lived here six weeks and you don't even know where a goddamned spatula is?"

"What's the matter with you?" Jack said. "I'm cooking dinner, for Christ's sake."

I wanted to read them what I had written so far, but the ink was smeared.

Acting class was in a loft above a stained-glass store, up a dark flight of stairs and through a thick sliding door.

The floor, high ceiling, and walls were all black. The air was filled with a certain reverence, like I had just entered a pagan cathedral.

A single black table sat in the middle of the stage, with a yellow pad on top and an empty glass. The yellow pad made me think of Frank, not that I didn't always think of Frank. A girl never forgets the first man she made love to.

The students were seated on folding chairs in the audience, while the teacher sat on the riser and leaned against the wall. She was in her late forties or early fifties, a small woman with gleaming blue eyes.

An incredible looking man walked on stage and for a moment I thought he was James Dean's ghost, he had such an attitude and glowed with such a wicked halo. He grabbed the table and pulled it back off-stage.

A few moments later when he sat down next to me, his aura was gone. He was just a plain kid in a leather jacket.

I knew then that the stage was magic.

"Today we will work on Place." The teacher, Fiona, spoke in a low, almost hypnotic voice. "Use all your senses and all of your concentration. Basically you're on your own. Listen for my voice out of the periphery of your consciousness. After a short period of relaxation, we will begin."

Each student carried a chair to the stage, sat down and let his or her arms dangle. Their feet spread out in front them, and their heads dropped to one side.

"Now, create a place," Fiona began. "A place familiar to you, that you have been to many times. I prefer you use an older memory."

I didn't choose the place, it chose me. A group of plaster of Paris chickens sat on top of an air conditioner. A rooster made out of corn, sunflower seeds, and macaroni hung on the wall.

"First, concentrate on smell. Memory is quickly retrieved through the sense of smell."

Biscuits and steaming greens and creamy corn, navy beans with thick-skinned bacon and a platter of the brightest red tomatoes anyone ever saw.

"Take the next few minutes to look slowly around the room at every minute detail, the color of the walls, the furniture, the curtains...."

Grandma's curtains looked like stale candy, mint green, and lavender butterflies. A big plastic cross and Jesus spelled out in Popsicle sticks hung beside the window. Grandma's kitchen was always full of chickens and crosses.

A plaque I made a long time ago in Vacation Bible School sat in the middle of the table on a miniature easel. It said: "Prayer Changes Things."

"Okay, that was a good day," said Fiona's distant voice.

From my imaginary window, the barn wasn't red anymore and the farm looked smaller than I remembered, like Disneyland gets smaller as you grow. At first it's endless and magical, then all of a sudden you see the dirt and the machines that move everything, and you find out the animals don't really talk.

"It's time to bring it to a close," said Fiona. "Now let's learn to come back, half the work is coming back...."

The first audition went well. It was a scene in which Veronica recites the 23rd Psalm "Yea, though I walk through the valley of the shadow of death, I will fear no evil: For thou art with me; Thy rod and thy staff, they comfort me." She recites this while her therapist kisses her neck.

I read it with a female casting director, a desk between us. It was not easy. It took everything I'd learned at Fiona's.

When I finished, she gave me another scene to study and said they'd have me back in two weeks for a screen test. I tried not to get excited.

"It's what I've always wanted for you," Mom said. That was the first I'd heard of it. She'd studied acting quite a bit and I think her divorce was a career move. But after the divorce, she was so busy trying to get married again that she almost forgot about acting.

I loved it that Veronica was supposed to be a Bible freak. I read the New Testament and memorized verses reciting them to myself as I delivered my lines. I locked myself in my room and did exercises from a book Fiona gave us, like holding imaginary oranges in my hands and feeling wind on my face and walking through make-believe water. Pretending I was surrounded by beautiful white clouds made me feel more graceful and feminine than I really was.

In THE COMFORTED, Veronica's father dies and she falls in love with her high school shrink and sleeps with him, even though she's a Jesus freak. Later in the script, the shrink tries to break up with her and Veronica is devastated. I read about how to substitute events in my own life to help me relate. I decided to use Frank leaving.

"How could you?" I said as Veronica, imagining I was talking to Frank. But instead of crying, "How could you?" came out as a big long angry scream.

It's so much easier to feel when you aren't confined to being you.

The screen test took place on a Friday morning. We drove past the golf course in Rancho Park, the top down on Mom's old Cadillac. The wind blew her straw-blond hair back like a lion's mane. The thick rims of her new red sunglasses rounded upward like arched eyebrows.

"I bet it shoots in Paris. Paris in the springtime. Wouldn't that be

30

fab? They'll hire a driver for us, a limo. They do that. I just hope Jack doesn't fly over, he gets so jealous of directors. We'd better go over your lines again."

"I know them fine," I said. "It's so creepy that I have to kiss a stranger."

"Honey, it's Dick Rand! God, if you're ever going to kiss somebody, he's the guy to kiss. I'm sure it's a far cry from some wet behind the ears...Shit." Mom stopped the car in the middle of the road. Her gas meter was in the red.

"How could you?" I said. "Didn't you see it was empty?"

"Oh, I don't know. I thought we'd make it."

She opened the door and stood up and pushed with both hands on the windshield until we started to coast.

We went about five miles an hour until a cop pulled us over.

"I was once in love with a police officer," Mom said as he came up to the window.

"Where were you going ma'am?"

"Nowhere, that's why I broke up with him." Mom laughed but the officer didn't.

"I'll help you push this over to the curb," he said.

Mom steered while he pushed us to a parking place between a couple of palm trees that looked like toothpicks reaching into the sky.

"Can you help us get some gas?" I said.

"There's a station about a mile from here."

"How are we going to get there?"

The officer just shrugged. "Triple A?"

"Can't you take us?"

"'Afraid I can't. Insurance."

He drove off.

"I hate driving that ten-year-old car," Mom said as we walked down Motor Avenue. "Jack's going to have to cough up the Jaguar he promised. I'm so mad at him. Maybe we'll get this movie and buy it ourselves, how about that?"

We stood at the stage door, wondering which way to go and who to talk to. We were an hour late and we both had arms full of clothes we'd been instructed to bring. The soundstage was dark and huge, and echoed like the inside of a whale.

I looked up at the ropes and rafters that hung from the ceiling, and up and down the walls like a shipwreck with cave fish swimming through portholes.

We finally found some pasty-looking people standing around a coffee machine, and approached a woman with a pencil behind her ear and a clipboard in her hand.

"We're here to see Don Richard. For the test."

She acted like she was thrilled to see us. "You're.... Angela?" she asked.

"No, Sean."

"We'll have to get you changed," she said. She spoke into her walkie-talkie as she led us to Don, who was surrounded by people. When Don saw us, he chuckled and threw out his arms, more like he was shrugging than offering a hug. Mom went to kiss his cheek like she'd known him for years and they awkwardly bumped noses as Don went for the other cheek.

Then he got business-like, thumbing through the stack of clothing we'd brought. He was slightly overweight and probably middle-aged, even though he still wore tennis shoes. He held up a yellow sundress and shook his head with a curious disapproval. He smelled of cigarettes and coffee.

Another woman came in carrying a box full of bathing suits. Don rummaged through the box, chose a bright pink bikini with the tag still on it and handed it to the blue-jeaned woman. He turned to offer Mom his tall director's chair, and as she sat down he winked over his shoulder at the wardrobe woman, pointed with his head and clicked his tongue like giddy-up. The woman led me away.

"We need to get you dressed right now," she said. "No make-up, he wants you natural." We moved into a large dressing room. She ripped the tag off the bathing suit and handed me the very tiny v-shaped bathing suit bottoms. It was time to undress.

Her hands were cold as she tied the straps of the top and then re-tied the corners of the bottoms so that the bows were more even.

Bright lights surrounded the floor-to-ceiling mirrors. I looked white and naked in the bathing suit. Goosebumps ran up and down my skinny arms and naked midriff. The pink of the bathing suit made me appear even paler than I was.

"You ready?" said the woman with the walkie-talkie.

The set was supposed to be a patio in front of the ocean. A bunch of reflectors and a large movie camera were pointed at a girl my age with long blond hair, wearing a bathing suit top and jeans. Her hair was thicker and longer than mine and she had a deep tan and full lips. She was so pretty. I looked at her long ballerina neck and thought, "Of course." If only I looked like that, maybe Frank would have never left.

Then I thought, Right, that's probably what Eva looks like.

Don Richard yelled action and Dick Rand took the girl into his arms. They indulged in a lengthy wet kiss before beginning their dialogue.

"I decided that we must stop seeing each other," said Dick Rand, between kisses.

"Don't be silly," she said. "God wants us together."

She stroked his chest and they kissed some more. It was embarrassing to watch. The girl let Dick Rand feel her up. I swore I would never do that again.

They did a whole five-minute scene, concluding with Veronica's "How could you?" She delivered all the lines I'd memorized with a wonderful thick pout.

Mom was watching, too. As soon as Don Richard yelled, "Cut," she laid a towel over my naked shoulders.

"You're much better than that girl," she whispered.

Up close, the set was ratty, like the patio of a cheap house someone rented who didn't plan to stay long. I sat on a rattan chair with
flowery pillows on it, beside a half-dead palm plant sprayed with oil
to make it look fresh.

A crewman put a cigarette out on the floor. Then he pulled a tape
measure from somewhere on the camera and stuck it under my nose,
measuring the distance from me to the camera.

While they adjusted the lights, I tried to go over the lines in my
head. It was difficult to concentrate. I couldn't tell if I was more nervous about the scene or the kiss or getting the job.

I was taken by surprise when Don suddenly said, "Okay, roll
'em."

I was alone in front of the camera. Dick Rand was nowhere near.
I started to panic.

"How are you doing, kid?" Don said.

"Fine," I said. A huge tin foil reflector shone onto the couch, just
to the left of my face. I couldn't see Don.

"Okay, baby, I'll talk you through this," he said.

"Where's the other actor? Who will I do the scene with?"

"He had to take a break, so we'll do something a little different.
Why don't you stand up?"

I stood up and moved into the warmth of the light. "Let's pretend you're taking a hot shower. That light's the uh, how do you call
it, spickit, sprocket? Water, where the water comes out."

At least it was a chance to use my sense memory. I turned on the
water and adjusted the temperature. I closed my eyes and felt it. The
hot water ran down my face and neck and chest.

"Good, good. I believe it," Don said. "Let out some sounds."

I had never vocalized in the shower, but in front of the camera,
with Don Richard's encouragement, I allowed myself to drift away
into imaginary steam and a deep satisfied sigh.

"Purrfect," said Don. "Oh yes, more of this..."

He held the camera on me for a long time, so I stayed in the shower, allowing imaginary water to drip down my neck and chest. It was heavenly and noises came out of me like I had tasted the most incredible chocolate known to man.

Don Richard finally yelled cut. "Thanks, baby," he said, snapping his fingers for the next girl. "We'll let you know."

Way to leave a girl naked, wet, and waiting. "Thank you, Mr. Richard," I said. But he was already busy with the next bikini.

5

The Lonely Moral Moonfrog

I HATED THE NEW HOUSE, even if it did have a pool. The carpet was so white you couldn't eat anywhere near it, and I wasn't allowed to tape posters on my bedroom wall. There was a view, supposedly the most important thing in L.A., but I didn't know why because you couldn't see lights or hills or ocean or even sky for that matter. Most of the time it looked like you were floating alone on a dirt cloud.

We'd lived in the old house on Le Doux for so long that we had accumulated seventy-four boxes full of possessions. Mom insisted we keep everything. Jack moved in with just his suitcase and a Porsche.

I was supposed to unpack half of the boxes, stuff I had no idea what to do with. Clothes I'd outgrown, Barbie dolls, diaries, photographs I'd taken of Mom and Dad, like the one last Christmas when he bought her the fur coat she'd always wanted. She posed in it, smiling, with her head thrown back and her wisdom teeth showing. It was 90 degrees that Christmas and Mom was sweating in her new fur coat.

The last time we went back to the old house for more boxes, there was a delivery boy waiting at the door. His envelope was addressed to me, and it contained another script with pink and blue pages added to it, a shooting schedule and a contract.

It helped. I didn't have to think about moving anymore and everyone was being nice to me. Maybe they would be, I hoped, from now on.

Don Richard sat in his office, at his large desk, in front of a framed photograph of himself with a very young Jane Fonda. Beside us, on his large private patio, was a life-size statue of a Guernsey cow.

The director slid a stack of papers across his desk to us and lit up a Gauloise. Mom looked them over and we both signed all five copies. Then she pulled the pink pages out of her purse and glanced at them.

"This love scene doesn't require her to, um, undress," she said. "Does it?"

Don put his cigarette down in the ashtray in front of him. He put the tips of all ten fingers together, so his hands were like two spiders. He stared up at us through his eyebrows and the smoke.

"I think you would be wise to trust me. Leave it in the director's hands, no?"

"I just don't think, I mean, she's underage, I don't know...." Mom started to say.

"Little bird," the director was speaking to me. "Could you excuse us? Trust me alone for two minutes with your mother?" He smiled, delivering this last line to Eudora.

Mom looked slightly panicked and desperate for my approval.

I winked at her as I closed the door.

My mother said that a William Morris agent had the power to change your life from top to bottom. She completely abandoned unpacking and started to prepare for the appointment Don Richard made for her. She dusted off a monologue she'd learned years ago in acting class and went to work on it.

"You want to know the truth?" she yelled toward the swimming pool with one hand on her hip.

"Mom, why don't you use me as the other character?"

"Sean, don't stop me, I was into it. I'm using an imaginary person, standing right over there."

"On the water?"

"Can I please go on? Do you mind?"

Mom took a deep breath, closed her eyes for a moment, and continued with her scene. "I met him in a bar, that's where. He followed me and we lay behind the seats in the cinema. And I'll tell you the truth." She raised her face to the sun and closed her eyes, her sense memory making tears that she pretended to try to stop. "I loved him, damn it! For five minutes I loved!"

"That's great. Wow," I said clapping.

"Damn it, Sean. I wasn't finished."

"I never knew you were so good!"

"Well, thank you," Mom said and stood up a little straighter, calming down. Her eyes got clear and shiny. She was proud.

When she came home from the agent's office Mom went straight to her room with a bag of potato chips. She took off her high heels and got under the covers with her stockings still on. She picked up a Cosmo and pretended to read.

"Well?" I said. "What happened?"

"Do you know that Don Richard said that they're going to send us to the Cannes Film Festival? Can you believe it? Yachts and premieres, gowns, paparazzi..."

"What happened with the agent?"

A dark and gloomy cloud settled on Mom's face.

"I lied," she said in a monotone. "I told him I was twenty-nine."

"That's okay, you look young enough."

"You know what that agent said to me? He said: 'You're talented, but thirty-year-old women don't work. I have several of them, they never work.' "

Tears ran down her face, this time for real. Not her usual hysterical dry sobs. She didn't even make noise, just silent tears.

"I guess I'm all washed up. I never even got started and now I'm all washed up."

"Don't say that. Mom."

There were lines around her mouth, creases on her forehead. She definitely wasn't as beautiful as she used to be. I prayed that I would never get that old.

"Don't tell Jack, okay?" she said. "We'll just say I changed my mind. I never went." Mom closed her Cosmo and offered me some chips. "I'll tell him that I decided that my job is to take care of you and him. He'll like that. And it's true, it is really true."

The sound stage was dark and there were no windows. Every day I'd get there at seven a.m. and leave after dark. I'd lie back in a tall barber chair and the makeup artist would touch my face with warm sponges and big soft fluffy brushes. The hairdresser would brush my long hair and spend hours curling it and making it stay just right. I'd close my eyes and float away, and when I got up I'd look in the mirror and be so pretty.

But the days went by, and then the weeks, and I never worked.

"Why do they keep me waiting?" I asked.

"Well they have to pay you for six weeks, so I guess they figure... oh I don't know what's the matter with them," Mom said.

But she loved every minute. She sat in a high director's chair, and the grips and cameramen and assistants all flirted with her. She met other guys on the lot, too, people that could help her, producers and casting directors. She'd meet them for lunch at the commissary, or she'd call them up and say, "Oh, I just happen to be on the lot, shall I come by?"

After the pink pages, came purple ones, and after the purple, green. They rewrote the script to have the therapist dating several girls instead of just Veronica. Actresses arrived on the set at a rate of one per week. First a blonde, then a brunette, and then an Asian girl. Most of my scenes were either cut, rewritten, or assigned to another character. No fault of my own, Don Richard assured me.

Only two good scenes remained mine. The one where I cried at the therapist's office and then quoted the 23rd Psalm while he made love to me, and the one where he told me the relationship was over and I screamed, "How could you!"

I was determined to do the best work I possibly could. I spent long hours on the set working on my character. Using an exercise Fiona had taught me, I found a painting that could be Veronica and tried to make it come alive.

It was a girl with a round, flat face, eyes wide with confused awe, and an absolutely appalled frown on her face. It was painted by a patient in a mental hospital. It was called *The Lonely Moral Moonfrog*.

I couldn't wait to play Veronica. As I said the lines through the face of the Moonfrog, I could feel a total transformation, as if I was expressing something deep and primal and universal.

You can feel things when you're pretending you're someone else that you could never feel in real life. Love and pain stronger than you can imagine.

I was finally falling in love with something besides Frank.

On the day I finally worked, I buttoned my blouse to the collar. My mother watched from the chair that had my name on it.

I went over the scene in my head as the hairdresser brushed and ratted and sprayed my hair. Veronica is frightened that she's been called into school therapist's office, like maybe there is something wrong with her. The therapist asks why her grades are down. Veronica immediately starts to cry.

"My father overdosed and my boyfriend shot himself and all I believe in now is Jesus," was my line. "Jesus never cared about calculus or basketball or even seismic activity," Veronica says.

Then Dick Rand, the therapist, says, "Jesus cared about love." And a minute later they're on his desk, doing it.

Don Richard looked through a frame that he made with his hands, "Okay, so we'll take it up to Veronica's line: 'Yes, yes, Jesus did care, you are so right'," Don said. "After that, honey, I want you to get up and go around the desk. We'll cut to a two-shot with the girl and Dick. And we'll do the rest after lunch."

The make-up man finished my lips and I was ready when Don said, "Roll film." But before he yelled action, the assistant director came up and tried to blow something into my eye. He towered over me and smelled like tobacco.

"What are you doing?" I said.

"Menthol. For tears. Tilt your head." He put his hand on my forehead, pushing it back. My right eye stung.

I knocked his hand off my forehead. "Please stop."

He looked at me with impatient disgust. "C'mon honey, we don't have time to mess around. Director's orders. "

"I don't need it."

A voice came from behind the camera: "Look baby, I know, I know, sorry," It was Don Richard and he pretended to plead with me. "It's so close to lunch and we have to try to get this in one take. I want you to look beautiful and we need tears."

"Excuse me, Don," said a female voice from behind the lights. It was Mom. "She said she didn't need it," my mother said, quite firmly. "Sean's an actress. She'll give you real tears."

Mom laughed all the way to the commissary with some television actor. Right after Mom and I sat down Don Richard sent champagne to our table.

"Allow me," he said, as he filled Mom's glass and then mine.

"She's underage," Mom whispered.

"Nonsense," Don said. "In my country all children have wine with meals. Champagne is simply more special."

Don pulled up a chair and sat down. His cigarette made me choke.

"You sure smoke a lot," I said.

He ignored my comment and took my mother's hand.

"Darling, there is a man across the room who would like you to visit his set. You've heard of him? I told him you were an actress."

Eudora nodded toward the television actor. He was looking at us. Mom loved restaurants and this studio commissary was the ultimate.

Don turned to me. "And you, my small bird. This next scene is an important one."

"How was the last scene?" I said. "Do you think I did okay?"

"Fine, fine," he said. "But this is the one you can shine in. You've kissed a boy before, no?" I didn't like his grin. "But, I bet you haven't kissed a man, at least in front of a camera."

There was no point in telling him my boyfriend was a man. Oh how I wished I'd gotten a photo of Frank and me together.

"Are you ready?" Don Richard stroked my cheek with the backs of his cold fingers. "Are you nervous? Don't be."

"I'm not," I snapped.

"Bon," he said. He raised his glass. "Two fantastic women! Actresses and perhaps, stars!"

I toasted and drank champagne, and Mom didn't say a word when I poured myself another glass.

Don Richard lit another cigarette. He coughed, then winked at me. "Protects my lungs from the smog," he said. "May I walk you back?"

Dick Rand sat at the desk on the set of the shrink's office, framed therapy license on the wall behind him. He wore tortoise shell glasses and light colored pants, with a white shirt that bulged slightly open between the buttons.

I found him most unattractive. I had studied him carefully in an effort to justify Veronica's love and find a way to kiss him. He had one saving grace: his earlobes were shaped like Frank's. Small and puffy, like soft little pussy willows. It was something.

As the make-up artist powdered my forehead and the hairdresser spritzed me with hairspray, I focused on his earlobes and prepared for the big scene.

"Now just go with it, okay?" Don said, unbuttoning my top two buttons. "Whatever happens. Trust me?"

"Sure," I said.

"You're terrific." He clapped his hands. "Let's go. Roll 'em." Everyone was dead silent and focused on us. "Action!"

"I've been watching you," said Dick Rand, who was evidently in character, but never seemed like a therapist to me. "The way you... pray, your obsession...is so sexy..." He kissed my neck every three words. "...I grew this beard...especially for you."

My next line was a definite struggle as Dick Rand slowly unbuttoned my shirt.

"As I walk through the shadow of the valley of death..." he kissed my neck and on down my chest and I let him ".... I will fear no evil..." He pulled me to his chest and kissed me on the lips, and I pretended he was Frank and gave myself totally to the scene.

Dick Rand opened my blouse and pulled it down off my shoulders. The hot lights seemed to be getting hotter. As I finished quoting the Bible, I helped him take my blouse off.

When the scene was over Dick Rand didn't stop and no one yelled "Cut." I managed to stay in character, as Dick Rand huffed and puffed and rubbed my leg all the way up my dress to my panties. I was totally Veronica. I did my job and the camera kept rolling.

"Brilliant," Don finally shouted, laughing. "Absolutely brilliant. Let's save it!" He slapped Dick Rand on the back.

"That was inspired," said Dick Rand, wiping his forehead.

"She's wonderful, isn't she?" Don stroked my hand like he was in love with it.

"Thank you." I blushed as the wardrobe lady put a robe on me. I was having trouble getting out of character. I still felt a bit like the Lonely Moral Moonfrog.

"Oh, my little wild bird." Don said in a low growl, ruffling my hair as he passed. Then he yelled, "Okay, let's move it. Next set-up!"

I looked around for Mom, who I hadn't seen since lunch. I was anxious to see if she was proud of me or angry.

She wasn't even around.

I sat between my mother and father in the screening room with three producers and the director and a guy from the insurance company. They wanted us to sign something, because I was underage, saying the nudity was okay. I couldn't believe my mother had called my father.

When my scene came on the screen, I looked prettier than I really was. I thought about Frank, watching this somewhere in Mexico, kicking himself for leaving me.

"I see your grades are down," said Dick Rand as the therapist. "I'm wondering if something's wrong."

"My father overdosed and my boyfriend shot himself," Veronica said. My eyes looked beautiful and wet, perfectly needy. Watching it, I felt a surge of pride at doing something well.

Then Dick Rand kissed my neck and talked about Jesus.

A moment later, my dad shifted his position and coughed. On screen, my breasts were naked, pressed against the graying chest of the therapist.

I wished I hadn't sat right next to my father. My breasts were the size of buildings with Dick Rand's wrinkled lips gnawing at me. The scene lasted forever.

I wondered when the eclipse would be in Mexico. I needed to go there before this movie came out. Like now.

They finally turned off the projector. My father didn't move. He stared straight ahead, his hand over his mouth.

I kept my eyes to the ground, but I could feel Mom looking at us, as if to say, "I told you so." Whatever that meant.

The other men got up and stood over us.

"It's a real opportunity for her," said the producer. "Don Richard made stars of Marie Lalanne and Samantha Welles. He's famous for his women."

Dad's tongue moved around in his cheek like he'd bitten off something inside his mouth.

"It's a terrific scene," said Don. "She's wonderful in it."

The insurance man butted in. "It would cost us plenty to redo the day's shoot. You'd be held responsible."

Dad suddenly got up and went into lawyer mode. "Don't threaten me," he said. He shook his head. "I don't like the way you guys operate. I think you'd better mess with someone else. Let's go."

It was the first time I'd ever seen Mom follow him out of a room.

"Women have more power in the Jewish family," Mom was telling Dad. The traffic was terrible and it was taking forever. I was claustrophobic in the back seat of Dad's new Jaguar.

"Can they really sue us?" I said.

Dad looked like he had a migraine. "Hell, no. I don't know. I guess anyone can sue anybody for anything these days."

"Hey, what if I changed my name to 'Cristinas'?" Mom said, suddenly spunky. "With an S. Isn't that different? Eudora's so old fashioned. 'Cristinas.' It's beautiful."

A car slammed on its brakes in front of us. I braced myself on the back of the front seat, as our car screeched to a stop.

"Why didn't you honk, Craig?" Mom said. "For God's sake. The light was yellow."

"Can't you just make them cut the nude part and use my other two scenes?" I asked.

"I can't make them do anything," Dad answered. "I wish I hadn't even gone. I never wanted you in this business in the first place."

"The beginning of the scene was good, though," I said. "Wasn't it?"

"Craig, it's a green light, why don't you honk at them, the light's green. Honk!"

Dad honked his horn loud and long. "Damned idiotic street."

"You think I'll ever work again?" I asked.

"You never know in that business. Probably not, if we let them sue us."

"How do you roll down the windows in this stupid car?" Mom said.

"I can't think of any other way you could make that kind of money again," said my father, always pragmatic. "I guess we could tell them to just go ahead and flaunt your body all over the world."

"Did you think I was good?"

"Yeah," said my mother. "You were good." The tone of her voice didn't match the words and she looked like she wanted to hit me. Like it wasn't that I was naked that bugged her. It was because I was good.

The stress of the day suddenly hit me. I was sick to my stomach.

"Pull over," I said.

"What do you mean, pullover. He can't pull over, there are cars behind us."

I opened the door of the moving car and leaned my head out. I almost fell on the pavement as I threw up.

6

Elvis' Dune Buggy

"LEAVE A PAIR OF PANTIES in his bed," Julia said. "Black lace. He'll call."

"I haven't seen him for three months, Julia. I don't even know where his bed *is*. "

"Where does he sleep?" she asked.

"In Mexico. Somewhere."

"So go there and find him."

"Go to Mexico?"

"You're in love, aren't you?"

"Alone?"

"Just forget it. Come over. You won't believe where I'm staying. You'll never believe who's here."

"Okay, but don't I need a passport or something to go Mexico?"

"It's a third world country. They don't care who goes there. They only care who comes back."

I hadn't seen Julia since she left for London six weeks ago. Julia's folks were trendy shrinks who traveled all over the world, charging tons of money to get people to scream their lungs out. They'd all been flown to London by some rock star who had built a padded room especially for this therapy.

I finished the bottle of wine I'd been working on and slipped a pair of jeans over my white drug store panties. My folks were out of town and I had the car Don Richards had lent me. It was raining so I covered my head with a cardboard box and ran out to the dune buggy. It was lime green and all souped-up, with a Porsche engine and a gold plaque on the dashboard that said *Designed Especially For Elvis Presley*. Don Richard said he traded it from Elvis for angel dust.

I lit a cigarette while I warmed the engine and looked for the directions Julia had given me. I couldn't find them, but I remembered the address.

It was nearly midnight when I managed to find the house. The front door had a picture of an open mouth below the peephole, bright red, like someone was sticking his tongue out at you. I stood in the rain and knocked and rang and nobody answered. The door was unlocked, so I opened it.

The living room was large and hollow sounding, with terra cotta tiles and a huge grand piano that had been painted green. Gilded lions held up the beams, and small electric candles with moving orange flame lined the walls.

"Julia?" I yelled. "Julia?" I stopped short when I saw, on a dark velvet couch with overstuffed pillows, a man nodded out, his mouth wide open and an unlit cigarette hanging from his fingers.

"Wow," I said aloud. "That's Keith Richards."

He sat under a lamp with a purple light shade. He half-opened his eyes and looked down his cheeks at me. His mouth hung open like he was too tired to close it. Very slowly and carefully, he lit a match, but before he got it to his cigarette, his head fell back down again.

"Wow," I couldn't help but say again. He woke up suddenly, just long enough to shake out the match that was burning his fingers. He looked totally out of place in three dimensions, like he ought to be flat on a magazine page.

A loud crash on the floor above shook me from my stare. There was an old elevator in the three-story house and I heard a girl's laughter echoing down the shaft. I looked up the dark hole and pushed both buttons several times, but the elevator didn't budge. There was a long, curving, dramatic staircase and I took one step at a time, trying to be cool in case Keith woke up again and saw me.

"Hey!" Julia waved. She stood in the middle of a huge steamer trunk full of antique velvet and lace dresses that she had just knocked over. She looked wild, hair that went every which way and tons of bracelets and necklaces and eye shadow. "Come on," she said, laughing, throwing a black velvet coat at me. "Dress up."

"Great!" I caught the jacket and started to put it on, but my hand got tangled, ripping the lining. "Shit! Look what I've done. It's all ripped."

"It's okay," Julia said sweetly. "It's just a jacket. Here, I'll find you another one."

"God, I'm sorry I messed it all up."

Julia pulled herself out of the trunk and got her balance. " I need my feather," she said, "where's my peacock feather?" She disappeared into a walk-in closet, where more clothes were piled on the ground.

A young skinny guy, with a dirty black t-shirt came in from the bathroom, and grabbed a guitar he found leaning against the wall. "Hey, Julia," he said, "is this electric one of Keith's?"

"Damn it Chris, I can't find my peacock feather," Julia whined from deep in the closet.

"I can't believe I'm playing his fucking guitar!" Chris said shaking his head. "Fucking Keith fucking Richards."

I wandered into the bathroom. There were gold records up and down the walls and a bent, burnt spoon sat on the edge of the pink-tiled sink. I thought about how I would tell Frank about this, if he ever came back from Mexico. I would say Keith did drugs with us. I would say he played a new song he wrote and he flirted with me, but I was cool and ignored him.

"You look sad, Sean," Julia said. "You need to go somewhere. I know this guy who's going to Egypt to sleep in the great pyramid," she said, putting her fingernail in the powder on a folded piece of paper and holding it below my nose.

"No, thank you." I turned my head.

"You want to go? To Egypt? I could call him."

"I want to go to Mexico," I said.

Julia tossed a pile of clothes back into the closet and came into the bathroom. Her peacock feather sat on the toilet tank, broken right below the tip where all the colors got round.

Julia handled it like it was a stillborn puppy. "It's broken. It's so sad. My poor peacock feather." Tears filled her eyes and then she suddenly dropped the feather. "Let's really get down," she said.

"I wouldn't know how," I said.

Julia poured some of the heroin into the spoon. "I'll help you," she promised.

Chris leaned up against the bathroom door. "We'll all help you," he said. "We'll all help each other."

I picked up the book that lay open on the floor in front of the toilet. Someone had written in it. Maybe it was Keith. Maybe if I read what he read, that would help. "Hey, who underlined this?" I asked.

"What's it say?"

I read the quote aloud. "'There will come a time we shall be so enlightened, we will look with indifference at the crude, heartless drama life offers.'"

Chris stared at me in awe. "That is so damned heavy," he said.

I read on. " '...When we shall have closed up those lower, undependable instruments of thought, that are called feelings.' "

Julia lifted the rug and opened a small vault built into the floor. She pulled out a clean syringe, still in its hospital plastic.

"Come on, let's get down." She lit a match under the spoon until the liquid gurgled and boiled and then she dropped a ball of cotton into the spoon. She stuck the needle into the cotton and slurped the liquid up into the needle. She wrapped a satin paisley necktie tightly around her arm and made a fist. Then she stuck the needle into the soft crease of her arm.

"Chris, I can't find the vein, come help me," she said. Chris put down the guitar and took hold of the syringe, poking around until blood shot up in the dropper, filling it red. Then he plunged it slowly back into her body. I watched as her whole body relaxed and her eyes got dreamy. She smelled really sweet, like the dying gardenia behind her ear.

"You want some Sean? You ready?"

"No, I don't think so."

"You can just snort it if you're scared. Chris, make her a line."

Chris poured some out on the counter and rolled up a dollar bill.

"Do you have that Velvet Underground album?" I asked.

"Yeah, that's a great album," Chris said.

I purposely ignored the voice in my head and the finger that always stabbed me in the chest when I was doing something bad. "Just this once," I told myself. I took the dollar bill and sniffed up the brown powder.

It took a while, but I got off good. I loved the warm numbness, like floating in a bathtub, like neither your body nor your mind could bother you at all. I felt like an angel, like I was golden calm and my bones and flesh were soft flannel blankets wrapped around, protecting me.

The bed sheets were dirty gold satin and I woke up sometime in the night, beside Julia. A beaded lampshade didn't quite cover the hundred-watt bulb over the bed, so I got up and draped it with Julia's pink and black scarf.

"Look at her, she's so beautiful," Julia was saying to Chris. She wore a peach satin nightgown, antique, forties, and she looked like something out of an old movie, pretty and pouty, her arms reaching out to me. "Let me touch you, Sean," she pleaded like a small child. "Please."

The smoky pink light from the covered shade shone down on us like a soft eerie dream. "Kiss her, Chris. Please kiss her, please."

Julia touched my face with the inside of her wrist, soft skin, gentle and clear white. Chris kissed me on the cheek, then the neck, the chest, more to please Julia than for any other reason.

"Make love with her, Chris," Julia coaxed and pretty soon Chris was on top of me. I fell asleep just seconds later, Chris humping so slowly that he finally just rolled off between us.

I woke up under the silky Chinese quilt. The smell of Julia's scarf smoldering made me cough. I climbed over Chris and grabbed the burning scarf and rubbed it out with a man's shoe I found beside the bed.

The numbness had melted and, like ice held tight in the palm of your hand, it left my insides bone-cold and aching.

Neither Julia nor Chris woke up. They looked so still, that for a moment I was frightened. I moved Julia's unbrushed hair off of her face. She looked dark and strange, and felt cold and clammy. I licked my finger and held it below Julia's nose. Julia was breathing, but her skin had a gray pallor.

I looked in the bathroom to see if there was any more dope. The square of paper still had a pile of brown powder on it. I took a couple of snorts, and then folded it and put it in my pocket. Surely they had more.

The room had started to get light. I needed to get out of there.

Maybe Keith was awake. Maybe I could talk to him. Maybe that would make me feel better. I found my keys and went downstairs.

Keith still lay on the velvet couch, his head on one shoulder, his mouth wide open. A cigarette, burnt down to the filter, hung between his two yellowed, calloused fingers. He didn't hear me say his name. He didn't seem to notice when I went out the front door.

I drove up to Mulholland in the lime green dune buggy with all the windows down. My long hair flew into my face, "Do You Believe in Magic" played on the radio. I pressed down the gas, and whipped around those curves. I drove faster and faster, singing with the radio about magic and a young girl's heart.

The road disappeared and my mind was going faster than the dune buggy's Porsche engine. I wondered if Julia was okay and thought about what a very strange color she had been. Suddenly it didn't seem like such a good idea to have more of that dope. I thought about Frank and how he would have loved to meet Keith, and then I remembered him, playing guitar on the beach. I felt so safe with Frank.

I fumbled for the paper with the stash inside, it was in one of my jeans pockets. I had to practically stand up in the car and I hoped I didn't fly off a curve. The car veered near the edge of a hill and I slammed on the brakes, just in time.

I checked the rear view mirror. No one was coming, so I backed up and parked in the shoulder. I unfolded the paper and dumped the brown powder onto the gravel. I needed to go to the bathroom, so I walked a little way down into the brush and found a bush I could hide behind.

I stumbled over something, it was a pile of clothes, jeans and shirts, all black. I looked around for naked people, but no one was there. There were clothes for several people, not like a couple who were doing it in the bushes. Curious, I picked up a pair of jeans to check the pockets. They were stiff with something all over them and underneath them was a dirty white undershirt. The dirt looked like blood. They were covered in blood. I dropped the pants and ran.

My heart was going a thousand miles a minute. I ran back to the car and started it up. The news was talking about some grisly serial murder. I still had to pee, but never mind. I turned off the radio and drove.

7

Love, Frank

I GOT HOME AFTER FINDING those bloody clothes and my mom was gone, with a note saying that she'd be in the desert for a few days. I needed something to eat or drink or do, but nothing sounded good or filling or possible. My skin was closing in on me. I wanted to scream or hit someone. No one was home.

I put water in a pan, determined to think of nothing else, just stare at the water until it boiled. Steam formed quickly in my head, telling me how scary life was, how I was missing information, missing being held, missing something. I tried to concentrate on the water, but all I could think about was Frank and how warm I had felt when he was near.

My face burned from the steam. I thought about Jack and how I never told Mom he touched me, because she probably wouldn't have believed me anyway and she was happy with him, for better or for worse, whatever that meant. The water moved, but didn't boil. Oh God, what the hell was I supposed to do about that movie. It would break my Grandma's Baptist heart if she ever knew I posed half-naked.

I kept thinking about all this and my mind got more and more confused like a photo in developing chemicals except reversed, from the crisp image back to the grey smear. The only clear vision was that dreamy goodbye kiss and the postcard from Mazatlán with my two favorite words: Love, Frank.

The water broke into a big boil right before my eyes.

I phoned a taxi before I even thought about what to pack. Very little: a bathing suit, a few t-shirts, a Spanish dictionary, the birth control pills the doctor gave me for cramps.

My few belongings fit in a small duffle bag, and the cab pulled up as I zipped it closed. I took the hundred dollars Mom had left the maid for groceries. It wasn't stealing. I'd buy groceries. I'd just buy them in Mexico.

The driver met me halfway between the cab and my front door, which I'd slammed shut without even bothering to take my keys. I loved the idea of having few possessions, nothing to lose, nothing between the world and myself. It was like dancing naked in the woods.

The driver looked like he'd been up for days. His clothes were all wrinkled and his beard scruffy. I wondered if he realized his fly was undone. I hopped in back and felt like I was already flying as I said, "LAX."

I had meant to leave a note, but forgot. I wouldn't have known what to say, anyway. Bye, Mom? The further away I get, the less I miss you?

I played over in my head the conversations I'd had with Frank and all the clues as to where he might be. Still on the beach in Mazatlán or headed toward Chiapas, wherever that was, somewhere in the mountains, where we would watch the eclipse together on his twenty-first birthday. And then, God knows where we'd end up.

At the airport, I bought a one-way ticket. Coming back was only a vague thought, like a dark bird flitting through a shadow.

A woman's got to follow her heart, I thought, or she'll regret it her whole life.

8

Mazatlán, Mexico, August 1969

THE SAND ON THE BEACH had been warm the day before, but now it was burning hot. And the waves weren't soothing like I'd expected. They sounded like bombs exploding on the beach.

A skinny blond guy appeared out of nowhere, running backwards on the beach in front of me. He wore jeans with a faded Pep Boy's T-shirt. He thumped his chest with his thumb. I flipped my hair over my shoulder and walked fast, as if I had somewhere to go.

"Víctor, Víctor!" he insisted, as he tried to introduce himself. His skin looked strong and dark. Mine was sunburnt.

"I'm Sean," I said. "Sean Hayes." I was dying to ask if he knew Frank, but I was tired of the answer I'd been getting.

He held out his hand and I shook it. It was a playful handshake, like a quick little dance. When he let go, the palm of my hand felt empty and naked. I suddenly felt broke and alone in Mexico, which in fact, I was.

"¿Donde está a telephone?" I said.

Victor, the jester, danced around, his fist to his ear, a pretend telephone. He circled me like a puppy and laughed. "¿Teléfono? Vámos."

I followed him off the beach and into town, past people cooking on the sidewalk and signs that said Farmacia and Feliz Navidad. We walked through the large outdoor market, with its strange raw smells. Flies swarmed around red hunks of beef and pork. Women carried live chickens by their feet.

Across from the market was the Larga Distancia office. There were only two phones and both were in use. A woman crying in Spanish was on one phone, and on the other an Australian with a beer, talking to his mother or his wife, I couldn't tell which.

Victor waited outside while I gave the operator my number and tried to decide what I would say to my mom. All of my money was gone and I didn't know where I was going to sleep. I was almost ready to give up my search for Frank and go home.

I went into the dark cloth booth and waited for the operator to dial my number. The phone was warm and old-fashioned, and the ring sounded far away.

"Mom?" I had to shout so she could hear me.

"Where are you?" she asked.

"Mexico."

"Oh, Sean. Why on earth didn't you call me?" My mother started crying.

"I'm calling you now," I said.

"How could you do this to me?" Her voice spit rage and her tears had suddenly stopped. It dawned on me why I hadn't called sooner.

"The movie is coming out, the biggest thing that's ever happened to us, and you run away to Mexico?" She didn't wait for an answer. "All my life you've worried me..." She took a deep, loud, gasping breath that made me feel guilty, bored, and sad all at once. "When you were a baby, I worried about that fan and your little fingers. I always worried about my little fingers...."

"You mean *my* little fingers," I said, under my breath. She didn't hear me. She went on crying and yelling.

I could see the street through the slightly opened curtain. Victor stood on the corner, laughing with a man who held a goat in his arms. Staticky music blasted from someone's car. Life outside seemed vibrant and alive.

"You know what, Sean? It's not my fault." My mother's voice sounded more and more distant and strange. "I did everything I could for you, damn it. I hope you come back before the movie comes out. I told them you would, but there's nothing I can do. You make me crazy. I just can't deal with it."

There was a dial tone. I took a deep breath and felt a sinking in my stomach, like I was in an elevator that went up too fast, and only part of me went with it.

"I'm doing great," I said, placing the receiver carefully back in its cradle. "Thanks for asking."

I paid the receptionist with my last hundred pesos. Asking my mother for money would have been a bad idea anyway. She probably would have wired me a ticket home instead.

Outside there was dirt on the ground and hot dry air. Mexico was honest. I loved that. Here, when you made a long distance call it was a big deal, like home really was far away. And when you bought a chicken it was a whole chicken, feathers and all. It made a lot more sense.

I hadn't had breakfast and Victor invited me to lunch. We sat down at a small cafe in the middle of the marketplace. There were paper daisies on the plastic tablecloth, toothpicks and Nescafe on all three tables. Fruit was stacked in pyramids on the counter. Across the lane, the view from our table was the butcher. Severed cow heads, stripped of their hide, hung from huge metal hooks.

A large, soft, and smiling woman in a red dotted blouse and a pink flowered skirt waited on us. My bare feet were filthy, but she didn't tell me I needed shoes. A silver star shone on her left front tooth.

I ate what Victor ordered, tacos with something white in them.

"Good? No?" Victor was full of excitement, as if he was the one who was new to everything. His fingers were long and thin.

"What is this?" I asked. "What am I eating?" I pointed and shrugged my shoulders to communicate my question.

"Tacos de cabeza."

"What's that?" I took another bite. It tasted dry and sticky.

Victor got up and started chewing real loud and pointing to his head. "Cabeza, cabeza," he said.

I looked down at the white stuff in my taco and realized it was some cow's brain.

When I looked up at Victor, his face burst into a smile that I couldn't help but return. We both cracked up. Mine was nervous laughter about what I had eaten. I didn't have a clue what Victor thought was so funny, but it was still nice to laugh with someone.

I followed Victor down the block to a sign that read VÍCTOR: El VETERINARIO.

There was a painting of a pig beside the V for Victor and a picture of a dog above the El. A ladder leaned against the building.

"¿Qué te parece?" Victor asked, proudly pointing at his half-finished sign, asking me how it looked.

Just then a man drove up, honking his horn. He parked his noisy old flatbed truck in front of the shop and got out. Under his right arm was a Doberman puppy with big floppy ears. The man admired Victor's new sign. Then he handed the puppy to Victor and left.

I followed as Victor took the dog inside.

"Hey, do you know a guy named Frank, a musician?" I asked. Mazatlán was a small town.

"¿Un Americano? Sí. Vivió aqui por un tiempo pero cuando vino el circo, se fue con la culebradora."

"What?" I wasn't sure about my Spanish, but I thought he said, "Frank once lived here, but when the circus came, he ran off with the snake handler."

The shop was new, bright white, with an operating table in front of the picture window. There was one large room with a kitchen in back and a curtain behind that.

Victor set the puppy down on the cold linoleum and got busy laying instruments on his operating table. He looked more official when he put on his white doctor's jacket.

"Have you seen Frank lately?"

Victor's mouth turned down and his chin buckled in disapproval. "¡Ya, te dije! Se fue con una mujer. Eva."

"He left with a woman named Eva?" Just what I wanted to hear. Not only was he gone, he was gone with the other woman. Tattoo or no tattoo, he was back with his old girlfriend.

Victor asked me to put the puppy up on the table. He filled a hypodermic needle while I held the poor cowering dog. Victor pinched its behind and stuck the needle in, slowly depressing the plunger. By the end of the shot, the puppy was knocked out cold. He looked peaceful and relaxed. I wondered if that drug would work for me. Victor pinched the dog in several places with his suture, to make sure he was good and out.

"Dame tus manos," he said. I held out my hand thinking he was going to hold it or rub it on the animal's furry belly. "Aquí, aquí." He placed the Doberman's big soft ear between my fingers and drew a line on the inside of it, stepping back to look when he was finished, like an artist checking out his work. Satisfied, he picked up the scissors and cut off half the ear. Blood spurted out all over. The top of the ear lay on the table.

Victor pinched my fingers tighter. "Más fuerte, más fuerte." I held the two pieces of furry flesh together and watched large drops of blood spurt out of the ear and roll down my fingers until they dripped off my hand. Victor threaded a needle.

The bloody flesh of dog ear, soft as a pussy willow, kept slipping between my fingers. I held tight and closed my queasy eyes, but the image in my mind was even bloodier and more painful than the real thing. So I opened my eyes, stopped breathing, and shut off the part of me that couldn't bear it.

Victor sewed as if he were sewing two seams together to make a pillow. His long thin fingers guiding the thread made me dream of Frank, and the calluses I once loved, plucking at the strings of his guitar. I tried to concentrate, to focus on holding the ear-skin together evenly. I decided to ignore what Victor had said about Eva and pretended Frank was here, watching, admiring my cool detached skill and efficiency, like a doctor at a war site, turning this puppy into a better fighter.

Victor powdered the mended flesh with disinfectant and threw the tops of both ears into the trash. It was over. That was it. No fancy bandage like in the States. Cut, sew. Simple and straight forward.

He led me back to the bathroom to wash my hands. He stood behind me at the sink and ran his fingers up and down the curve of my waist. He moved my hair, slowly, then kissed my neck fast, like it was an emergency. My head fell to the side as pink water ran down the drain.

I looked across the room at the puppy, still lying unconscious on the operating table. I was hoping he wouldn't roll off the table. I hoped he would wake up.

Victor's bed was hard, just a one-inch thick mattress on top of a piece of wood, in a windowless room in back of his shop. The dog woke up in pain and yelped endlessly. It was a frightening cry. I stared at the ceiling, praying for him to stop.

Victor kissed each of my open eyes and tried to stick his tongue on my eyeball. It made me laugh. "You stay with me," he said. His English was suddenly, mysteriously better.

"I'm here, aren't I?" I said. I felt cool and powerful, like Frank had been with me.

"You work for me and have my baby," Victor said, smiling.

"I'll work for you, I need a job. How much?"

"You have my baby, too," he said.

"Yeah, sure," I said. I started to laugh and couldn't stop. Victor got mad and his face looked funny, like an animated gibbon. "I'd better go," I said, and that made me laugh harder because it was night and I was broke and I had no place to go.

Victor buried my laughs with kisses, and didn't seem to notice when I shut my mouth tight and disappeared into my mind.

When it was over, I scooted down under the sheets and put my head on his chest. My cheek rested gently on one male nipple and I lay there with a longing so deep I felt I might implode.

A lady with golden stars on her robes and golden rays around her face came to me in the night, spinning, flying, crying. She cut her eye and dripped blood into mine, the drops falling from her breasts like angry burning tears.

9

Elephant Milk

THE CIRCUS WAS IN MAZATLÁN and the elephant was having trouble giving birth.

Victor leaned both forearms on the steering wheel and peeled an orange as we drove out into the country. I stuck my thumb in the top of my orange and sucked juice out of the hole I'd made.

The window on the driver's side wouldn't open so Victor spit his seeds out my window. The first three flew past me, but the last two bounced off my face, a moving target since I was laughing so hard. Victor leaned over and kissed the tip of my nose, veering left after he barely missed an oncoming cow. I felt attractive. I'd distracted him from the road.

We pulled into a makeshift lot and parked among a dozen dust-caked trailers. A humongous muscleman met us at the truck and opened Victor's door. He wore a leather chest piece with metal studs, and black spandex pants slung so low they exposed his hairy belly button. Make-up whitened his face and highlighted his dark eyes.

"Curso," Victor said, shaking the man's hand as we got out of the truck. He introduced me.

Curso's mustache was black and grew long over his lips. I found him fascinating, but not attractive. Until he bowed and kissed my hand.

"Me encanta," he said, taking his time as he took in every inch of my face. I smiled back. I wondered if Eva, the snake handler, worked in this circus.

"¡Vámonos!" Victor said, as he lifted his doctor bag from the back of the pick-up.

Curso led us through the hot dust, past men working to raise a giant red and purple striped tent. The heavy smell of hay mixed with lion dung was rich and exciting. Tigers paced in cages and a lonely gorilla with sagging hairy breasts grabbed at us as we passed.

A small crowd had gathered around the elephant. Curso pushed us through to the center. A woman with curly pink hair and a long pink skirt stroked the elephant's trunk. "Lola, Lola, mi corazón," she said.

Victor took charge immediately, demanding water and clean blankets. "¡Agua, agua!" he shouted. " ¡Y sábanas limpias!"

The elephant knelt down on her front knees, as if she knew the doctor had arrived. She laid her wrinkled trunk on the ground. Her hind leg was chained to a stake, but she had managed to scoot around until her butt was high in the air above Victor's head. There was an unbelievably huge bulge under her tail, pushing against her thick hide.

I had never been so close to an elephant. She towered over me, even in a kneeling position. Her knees looked like gray monster knuckles, and her thick skin was covered with deep lines. Long soft hairs fell from her chin. Her belly contorted and swayed from side to side.

I walked carefully up to Victor, keeping a safe distance as I got behind the elephant, wondering if she'd kick like a horse should I frighten her. Victor pushed on the bulge under her tail, studying it.

"What can I do?" I asked him.

"Entrégame la grasa," he said. He pointed at his doctor bag, a few feet away. I had no idea what grasa was. But I wanted to help and I could feel the elephant's pain. I brought back a large syringe.

"No, no, no!" Victor shouted. He flailed his arms, telling me to get out of the way.

I backed into the crowd and a large woman bumped into me, splashing me with water. She carried two overfull buckets, hurrying back to Victor. A tiny man, with a stack of blankets higher than his head, waddled back toward Lola.

"¡Silencio!" yelled Victor, clearly the boss.

Not a soul spoke as Victor wet a blanket, and with it, cleaned the area around Lola's bottom and up between her hind legs. He got a plastic garbage sack out of his bag and stuck his arm inside of it. Then he took the lid off a can of Crisco and smeared it all over the bag with his arm inside.

He held Lola's tail out of the way with one hand while he slipped his other hand slowly into her.

The deep dusty silence was broken now and then by the sound of a metal pole being lifted, a lion's roar, a horse, a bird, someone shifting his weight.

Victor's arm disappeared deeper and deeper inside the elephant, until the huge protruding lips of her vagina were wrapped tightly around his bicep. Lola stood fairly still and sucked her trunk into her mouth like a big thumb comforting her.

Victor's eyes closed tight and his mouth was tense with the effort of feeling for something he could not see. A tall, sweaty blond man with a Madonna tattooed on his right arm hummed a low giggle and looked embarrassed. The Pink Lady paced and chanted something that sounded Latin and Catholic. She suddenly grabbed Victor's arm and tried to pull it out.

"Pobre Lola," she wailed.

Curso pushed her back and pointed at Victor. "¡Él es el doctor!"

The Pink Lady stood back by me, growling under her breath. The elephant looked toward us with one tiny worried eye.

Victor pulled his wet greasy arm out of Lola, who was now quite agitated. Her tail shook, her ears flopped, her tremendous body shifted back and forth. Victor took off his garbage-bag glove and got the giant syringe out again. He filled it from a bottle of liquid and shot it into a vein in Lola's ear, removing the needle slowly, then pressing on the ear with a towel, like you hold cotton on your arm after a shot. Everyone waited to see what the medicine would do.

"¿No tiene algo de comer?" Victor finally said. Curso yelled some orders and before long, a woman came with a tamale wrapped in tin foil and gave it to Victor.

Lola picked up some hay with her trunk and tossed it onto her head. She was starting to calm down. I inched up toward Victor.

"What are you going to do now?"

"Esperar," Victor said. He took a big bite out of his tamale. "Es lo unico que puedo hacer. Esperar por Dios." Wait. It's the only thing we can do. Wait for God.

I slipped away and walked toward the trailers. Maybe I'd find some clue about Frank and Eva. I didn't want to ask anyone with Victor around.

A noise in the brush startled me. I jumped, afraid it was a rattlesnake. A lizard darted between my feet, slid up the wall of a trailer and entered through a half-open door. I went up the steps and followed him inside.

The desk had a plaque on it that said EL GRAN CURSO. On the walls, were faded color photographs. Monkeys rode lions, girls hung by their hair, and in another one Curso lifted a big old Plymouth clean off the ground.

Behind the desk was a bathroom with no door. The walls were

covered with more photos, but none of a snake handler, and not one of Frank.

In a black-and-white picture that had been painted pink and lavender, Curso stood on top of an elephant, holding a much younger and thinner Pink Lady in the air. He held her with one strong arm, his hand between her legs under her little purple skirt.

I stared at the photo while I used the bathroom, and imagined life in the circus. I pictured a glamorous version of myself atop an elephant, long red hair curling down my back, toes pointed ballerina style, one knee bent and the other leg straight, like the beautiful Pink Lady in the photo.

"You like?"

"God, you scared me." I finished zipping up my jeans.

"Help yourself," Curso gestured to the pictures on the walls of both rooms. "Look all you like."

"You speak English?"

"My wife, Ana, her father was from Indiana."

I stopped in front of a poster that hung behind the desk. It was Curso, his head in the mouth of a lion.

"This is vulgar." Curso pointed at the photo and stared into my eyes. "For the audience. But to make one's arm move in a gracious curve and entice the animal to leap, that is worthy of my life."

He moved his arm in a slow gentle arc toward the ceiling and I followed his hand with my eyes.

I had always thought that the whole purpose of a circus was to escape, and pretend that everyone was happy, with clown grins and hearts as light as balloons. But then I saw the grace and concentration with which Curso moved his arm. At that moment, I knew the circus was much, much more. It was beauty, performance, and art. It was serious. Sometimes, even life and death.

Curso leaned on the top of the desk and studied me as he combed his mustache with his lower teeth. "Your hair. So red, so beautiful. You dance?"

"Ballet. When I was small."

"Have you ever been on stage?"

"Oh yes. I've acted." The thought reminded me of how much I loved pretending to be someone else.

"My show starts in one hour. I need someone. You want to work for me?"

"Really?"

"Perform for one week, maybe more? We travel. South."

"Are you going to Chiapas?"

Curso nodded.

"Don't I need to know how to do something?"

"You have body like a gymnast. I am good teacher. I pay you." He went to the door of the trailer and caught a stray worker running past. "Va por mi esposa," he commanded the man.

The Pink Lady came a few moments later. Her outfit showed lots of cleavage and her skirt was like a hip hugger, starting way down below her waist. She had flowers in her hair. "¿Me llamaste?" she asked.

"Take time from your elefante precioso to find costume for my new assistant."

She stared at him for a moment, then her eyes fell on me. She shrugged her naked shoulders and motioned for me to come.

Curso stopped me at the door. "Maybe you want to tell el veterinario first?" he said. "You work for him or what?"

"It wasn't a real job. I love performing and I need to travel."

"We leave here tomorrow. Maybe he is angry to lose you."

"Maybe," I said.

Ana, the Pink Lady, was silent as I followed her to the next trailer. It was dark and small and stuffed full, with clown costumes and Indian feathers and bright satin fabrics that smelled like mothballs.

She quickly thumbed through the racks of clothing and handed me a purple leotard, just like the one I'd seen her wear in the photograph, with a small frilly skirt and a pair of pink felt boots with tassels. She watched silently as I struggled to pull the costume up over my hips. It was tight, even though I was very thin. I tried to make a small joke of it, but Ana pretended not to speak English.

The purple skirt was short and I liked my long, slim, naked legs in the smoky mirror. Behind me in the mirror, the Pink Lady looked farther away than she really was, chewing the tip of one finger, her other hand resting on her stomach.

Lola's trunk stiffened and she kneeled, first on one knee, then the other. Every few moments, her belly tightened as her body pushed on the baby. Suddenly a ton of water poured out, like Niagara Falls, all at once. She doubled up with her weight on her hind feet and her trunk between her legs. She grunted and pushed until a huge white membrane full of liquid popped out. It hung there below her belly.

The Pink Lady ran to her side. "Bién Lola, bién," she said. "Good girl." Lola stretched one hind leg straight behind her. A wet baby elephant slithered out, fell onto its head and lay there stunned.

Victor and Curso rushed to the baby and dragged it away. Its naked squished face looked sweet and confused. Victor got a hand pump out of his bag and held it to the baby's trunk to suck the birth mucus out.

Several men leaned over the baby, their hands patting its belly and slapping its back, trying to get it to breathe. Lola watched, alone, eating what was left of the white placenta balloon. She looked out of the corner of her eye at the men hitting her baby.

When they finally got the baby to breathe, they put their hands under the huge creature and pushed and shoved and lifted. With a loud grunt in unison, the men got the baby up on its feet. It stood there uneasily for a moment, blinked its tiny eyes and tried to keep its balance. Then it fell forward, flat onto its nose.

Lola started toward the fallen baby, straining against her chains. Curso jumped up, and shouted, "No, no, Lola. No!" He hit her in the face with a stick.

"Why?" I cried, appalled at his cruelty.

"A veces, las madres matan sus bebes," the Pink Lady whispered.

"Kill their babies?" I asked, trying to understand what she was talking about.

Lola picked up a bunch of dirt with her trunk and flung it up into the air. She was mad. She did it again and again, spraying dust and little rocks all over everyone.

A wild-eyed man in red stripes started playing the fiddle in front of Lola's face. Curso shouted at him to stop.

Lola shifted her powerful body weight. Curso pointed his stick at her face. Lola raised her trunk, and let out a trumpet wail. Then she looked straight at me, desperately, as if saying, "Can't you please, please help me?"

"She needs her baby," I said. "Let her see her baby."

Victor sighed deeply and shook his head. "¿Qué tienes?" he asked, abruptly and loud. I understood that to mean 'What's wrong with you?' I was trying his patience.

The baby finally struggled to its feet by and headed toward Lola's tits. Lola looked back at the animal that had just come out of her and let out a terrific howl. Then she picked up one of her front legs and kicked the baby, knocking it ten feet back.

The sun was mean, getting lower in the sky and beating hot into our eyes. A line of people formed outside the ticket booth and the fiddle player entertained them. The performers changed into their costumes, bright shouting colors, and the band was warming up in the tent. The whole place vibrated with energy, circus people ran every which way, carrying things and shouting orders.

Curso explained my simple job: to enter running, stand on the other side of the far platform, and every time the drums rolled, point dramatically with my whole arm. He made it sound so important.

"You must entice the audience, you must use your arms and your smile to direct their eyes. You must make them know something is about to happen."

"Okay."

"Tonight, you will signal my entrance, tomorrow you learn more."

I tried to memorize exactly what Curso told me. Point when he enters and takes a low elegant bow. Point when he gets under the Plymouth and point when he lifts it above his head and point again when he takes another bow and leaves. Gesture, not point. I make grand gestures. Then I bow.

"Tomorrow, we rehearse." Curso curled his mustache between his thumb and forefinger. "Tomorrow, more for you to do. Acrobatics, tigers, okay? Maybe knives."

Meanwhile, Lola wouldn't give her baby any milk. Wouldn't even let her get close. The baby tried three times, struggling to take small steps. Lola knocked her back down, again and again.

Victor put a pail under Lola and pulled on her big nipples as if milking a cow. Nothing came out. He yanked harder and faster at her tits until finally we heard some deep splashes in the pail. The Pink Lady put the small bit of milk into a baby bottle.

We fed the bottle to the little one. The baby sucked eagerly and the milk was quickly finished.

"¡Más, más!" said Victor as he put the pail back under Lola. He pulled at her tits and Lola shifted her weight. Her ears flapped and she anxiously stomped her feet. Victor backed way off.

"¡Pinche elefante!" he said. "¡No puedo!" He just couldn't do anything with the damned elephants, and he was getting good and frustrated.

The Pink Lady was able to approach and managed to calm Lola down, stroking her trunk and whispering in her ear. Lola had been calm for several moments when Curso came towards us shouting.

"¡Vámanos!" he yelled, clapping his hands. "The show must go on!"

Ana jumped and stared angrily at her husband. The few circus people that had been watching scattered in different directions.

"Come, Ana," Curso commanded.

"I stay with Lola," she said.

"You come with me! You work."

"I stay with Lola."

Curso gave her a fierce look, snapped his fingers at me. I didn't know what to do.

"See you later," I said to Victor, avoiding both his and Ana's eyes as I followed Curso to the tent.

Three red metal platforms were in the ring and three lions paced in a hot pink cage. A huge spotlight shone back and forth over the ring.

I stood by the benches while the audience crowded in. The seats filled quickly and the tent was incredibly noisy. A man with a shiny bald head sold boxes of cajeta, or caramel, and Chiclets. My body tingled with anticipation.

The announcer spoke excitedly into the mike. The sound was garbled, but everyone cheered. Children crouched on the ground in front, heads darting back and forth as a clown ran into the ring dressed in red polka dots, chased by a zebra with a poodle on its back. A fat woman hula-hooped a ring of fire. Another clown followed, dropping his pants and miming an exaggerated laugh.

The tension grew in my stomach as I watched the acts leading up to my debut. First came the acrobatics, then the elephants, for a bit of relief. By the time, Lasse did his knife-throwing performance, my stomach and fists were both clenched. Finally, Ana's trapeze act was almost over and my entrance was imminent. I took a deep breath and tried to relax.

The drum made a rolling sound and the crowd grew silent. I

trembled with excitement, wanting desperately to do a good job. Curso poked me and said, "NOW."

I ran to the center of the ring and extended my arm to the wings, pointing back at Curso. The audience applauded furiously.

El Gran Curso entered with wide-open arms, parading his muscles and a lion standing on his huge shoulders.

I suddenly realized I was standing in the wrong place. I was where Curso needed to be. How could I be so stupid? Curso grinned at the audience as I scooted quickly past the platforms into position. It felt like everyone in the audience was staring at me and knew that I only had three directions to remember, and I had already fouled up one of them.

Curso arrived at center ring and threw out his arms, triumphantly ending his first moment. I breathed again, relieved, but only for a second. Because there was no Plymouth. There were only lions.

The audience yelped and clapped. The lion jumped off and ran to the platform near where I stood. She licked her paws, and I could hear her tongue lap and feel her breath like hot steam on the side of my face. Curso opened the gate, and two more lions zipped past him and took their places on the other platforms. I smiled at the crowd, trying to act cool and wondering what the hell I was supposed to do next. I was on my period and double terrified because I'd heard about sharks and blood. What if the big cats thought I was raw meat?

Suddenly the lion next to me started growling and a cold chill ran through me. I tried to steal a glance at Curso, while keeping my eye on the animal at the same time.

"Go, go," Curso hissed. I backed out slowly, smiling at the audience.

The crowd cheered. Curso dragged me back on for a bow. First he bowed with me, then I gestured as he bowed. And once more, we bowed together. It was so much more exciting than doing movies. I was bathed in applause. I felt its warm glow fill my body. I was high.

The sky was purple, almost dark. Screaming children were loaded onto the last visitor bus. The dust was littered with candy wrappers and burst balloons.

"The first thing you must know," Curso said, his arm around me like a big brother's as he walked me toward the trailers. "When a lion makes noise, it is good. When she pouts - Cuidado. That's danger."

Curso looked bigger than ever, still filled with applause from his show. His chest hair gleamed with sweat. He showed me to my new room. There were four bunks in the small, dark trailer. A deep purple light streamed in from the tiny window beside my bed.

If I did well, I could travel with the circus all the way to Chiapas, Curso promised. We would rehearse by day, perform during the evening, and travel in the night as we slept. I would be paid in pesos, the equivalent of twenty-five dollars a day, a lot of money for Mexico. He would train me to do gymnastics and work with the lions.

"Isn't it dangerous?" I asked.

"Yes," he said, his smile exuberant. "Very."

Victor sat on a stool next to the baby. He had his head in his hands and I couldn't see his face. I went up and stood beside him. I stroked his head as he fingered the skirt of my costume.

The baby elephant looked so very weary, like she'd been alive and suffering for thousands of years. One teeny eye blinked slowly as I sat down beside the limp little creature. I tried to put its head in my lap, but it was too heavy.

"No puedo hacer nada," Victor said. There was nothing he could do for the baby. Lola had finally allowed Ana to milk her but the baby had refused the bottle.

Victor got up and stretched and grabbed his bag. "Vámos."

I shook my head no.

"Es tarde. Vámos!" he said again. It's late. Let's go.

I shrugged my shoulders. "I'm going with them. I've joined the circus."

Victor stood there and stared at me, puzzled and hurt, like I had betrayed him. My nose got a tickle in it and I looked away, down toward the ground. Victor grabbed my arm and tried to get me to look at him. I wouldn't.

Victor said my name, softly, then repeated it three times. I refused to look up. I was kind of smiling and I didn't know why. I couldn't help it.

Finally he let go of my arm, threw it down. Then he very politely said good-bye. I watched as he walked away.

Alone, under the stars, I closed my eyes and found tears burning in my throat. I could go for weeks without feeling like that. It was a feeling I tried to avoid. Not much different than the way I'd felt on the beach, when Victor found me, or at the airport, when I said good-bye to Frank. Only tonight, it was harder to brush off. The tears were hotter and the silence echoed. Something about so many stars. You don't see skies like that in Los Angeles. The lights and the smog cover them up and make the night sky a sickly orange. Here the sky was a clear open space.

Ana, the Pink Lady, came quietly and knelt below Lola's trunk, a rosary in her hands. Her face looked soft, like the belly of a lizard.

I wanted to reach out my hand and touch the underside of her chin which curved gently as a rose petal.

The moon glowed in her eyes and I wanted to talk. I wanted to ask where she came from and if she had children and what it was like and if she ever prayed and what happens when we die and what are we doing here and in general, why?

I tried these questions in my head, but didn't ask. Because it was so nice and warm, sitting beside someone who just might know.

We sat side-by-side, and nothing changed but the moon which slowly came from behind a cloud. Lola stood silent, her large behind facing both us and her newborn, who lay in the dirt.

"Why doesn't she like her baby?" I asked.

"She just doesn't know," Ana said softly, speaking to me in English for the very first time. "She was born in the circus. She's never seen a baby."

Ana got up. She lifted her hand slightly, palm to the sky, fingers pointing towards my heart. I felt that if she touched me I would turn to cool white steam.

She leaned down for the blanket that lay beside me and with it, covered the baby.

"You think she'll live?" I asked.

"¿Quién sabe? Solamente Dios." Who knows? Only God.

Ana knelt beside me and wiped my wet cheek with the palm of her hand. She smelled like flowers and elephant milk.

10

Circus Arts

I WAS IN LOVE WITH the way Ana swung upside down, her legs wrapped around the ropes of the trapeze, her pink curls streaming down, her body still strong and beautiful. She'd pick up momentum until the next trapeze flew her way and then she'd grab it, circle around until her belly reached the bar, and balance there, her arms spread slightly back, like a gliding feathered jet.

To me, El Circo de Gran Curso was better than Barnum and Bailey because it was small and none of the performers were specialists, everyone did several jobs. Nothing looked out of reach. Ana was just a woman flying high above the ground, not perfect, just great.

During the day the tent was empty, except for the performers and the animals, working out their acts. It felt serious, and I didn't mind that Curso was fierce and temperamental while he worked. He wanted to accomplish something, to make his show better and better. I'd never seen anyone so intense. He swore I could learn.

"You must be devoted, joyful," Curso told me, his black eyes flaming. "You must play with the passion of a child."

Behind him, Ana swung back and forth in a gentle whir of sound and a soft blur of pink.

"To make it look easy is beautiful, yes?" Curso said, gesturing toward Ana's trapeze. "Nothing is easy. You must work hard at gymnastics and make friends with the lions. And you must listen, always listen to me."

Ana jumped off the trapeze and onto the platform, and her deep joyful laughter was private and full of pleasure at what she'd just done.

With one thick finger under my chin, Curso turned my face toward his and lowered his eyes to mine. The low timbre of his voice reminded me of Frank. His passion hit deep in my body.

"If I am hard with you, I tell you this now: I am sorry. It is for only my Circus."

I sat cross-legged on the ground outside the ring and watched, waiting for my turn to rehearse. Workmen carried in large wicker hampers and when they finished with the trapeze, Curso began to open the hampers one by one, pulling out larger and larger snakes. He spoke to them in Spanish and petted each one. He held a python that was thicker around than my thighs.

I hoped he did not plan for me to take over the snake handler's job. Not that I was afraid of snakes. They simply didn't interest me.

No. I imagined myself flying through the air on a trapeze or balancing on top of an elephant, looking elegant and proud. I saw myself gesturing, enticing a tiger to jump through a ring of fire. I heard the cheers of thousands and fantasized about Frank, one day, wandering around some small Mexican town looking for coffee. He'd stop dead in his tracks and stare at a poster, tacked onto an electrical pole, advertising the dates the circus was coming and beneath: a large picture of me, riding high atop an elephant.

"Wow," he'd say to himself, "that's incredible." He'd break up with Eva and wait for weeks, until the circus came. He'd take a shower first thing that morning, then buy his ticket and wait for show time. He'd watch from the audience and say, "That Sean is really something." Then he'd come backstage to find me.

My eyes were closed when I felt Curso above me.

"You are not paying attention?" he said.

Right as I looked up, a snake snapped its awful forked tongue right in my face. A diamond shaped head touched my cheek, and as I jumped and tried to move away, another snake swiped my neck with its creepy crawling body.

Curso had wrapped five or six of them around his neck. Their heads jutted out several feet and their strong bodies slinked around in front of me and snuck up behind me. Goosebumps covered my arms and legs.

"Relax," Curso said, laughing.

"I am relaxed," I said. "I'm ready to rehearse."

Rehearsal went from dawn until noon and started again from three to five. Just like making a movie, most of my time was spent waiting. Only here there were real animals to pet and make friends with. I instantly trusted Enrique, the young male elephant, more than I trusted the men on a movie set.

Curso and Lasse, the knife thrower, did tricks on the back of Enrique. Lasse was blond, a tall Swede, younger and slimmer than Curso, but not as strong. He had a wide forehead and a classic nose, and reminded me of a Greek statue with a tan.

Together, the two men lifted Ana above their heads, parallel to the elephant. Then they let go, and she supported herself, her hands on Curso's shoulders. Her arm muscles bulged, her entire body was taut with her legs pointed straight back, ballerina-style while Lasse let one ankle rest in his raised hand.

I sat alone and clapped after every act, until finally, in the late afternoon, Curso snapped his fingers and I ran into the ring. I was told to just relax and do as Ana did.

Ana stood by Curso's side, so I took my place on his other side. Curso rolled his shoulders, then bent down and placed his hand between my legs. He slowly lifted us, one woman on each hand, like hundred pound weights. Ana pointed her toes and arched her back like she had done when he lifted her alone on top of the elephant. I tried to strike a pose like hers, but wavered a bit and upset the balance.

Curso put us down and turned to me. "You must relax, relax." He put his hand between my legs. "This time I try you alone," he said.

He lifted me up as Ana stood watching and I struggled to look graceful. "There, that's the way," he said, quite satisfied. "Very good, good." He wiggled his fingers in my crotch, adjusting his grip. His hand was warm. I held my back straight and concentrated on my balance. I was determined to be good at this.

When he set me down he patted me gently, on the crotch. "Nice," he said, drawing the word out long before he removed his hand.

Ana shot one quick glance my way, then looked out to where the audience would later be and smiled.

I headed toward my trailer to change from my costume, back into my jeans. The light footsteps behind me turned out to be Ana.

"I'm going to feed the elephants," she said, in a rushed half-whisper. "Like to come?"

Out back of the trailers, Lola was chained to a stake in the ground. She ate from a burlap bag that was ripped open and full of half rotten apples. The thick veins in her ears seemed to pulse as we approached, but she didn't look our way.

The baby still hadn't eaten and was getting very weak. She lay there chained to a separate stake. Lola ignored her.

"Does the little one have to be chained too?"

"She must get used to it."

Ana poured a can of human infant formula into a big bottle. Only once had the baby elephant tasted her mother's milk, the one time Lola had let Ana milk her. Ever since that first time, Lola had slapped Ana with her trunk whenever she got too close, just as she slapped her baby.

Ana gave me the bottle and I held it to the baby's mouth, but the baby refused to suck. Ana had already tried sugar water and cow's milk and the baby didn't want those either. I held the nipple above the side of her mouth, letting drop after drop fall onto her lips. She licked them with her tongue, but didn't seem too interested.

It was difficult to tell in a baby elephant, but Ana decided that she was female, which made it all that much more important that she live. Males are more expensive to feed and become very difficult once they reach adolescence. Male elephants have a cycle, almost like a woman's. Once a year for a couple of weeks they tend to get violent.

"They are only held by the illusion of their chains. When they break loose, they are very dangerous."

"Those chains aren't strong enough, are they?"

"Only when the elephant is very small. And then, when they grow up, they don't seem to notice that they've grown stronger than their chains."

We sat there patiently while drops of milk continued to form on the nipple and drip into the baby's mouth.

"What will we name her?"

"Popalotl," Ana said. "Butterfly. See?" Ana lifted the baby's ear. "Like butterfly wings."

"Popalotl. Is that Spanish?"

"Chol. My grandmother's language. She speaks little Spanish, much less English."

"But your father was from the States?"

"Yes, I was born there. But when I was five, my mother started crying and didn't stop until my father sent us home to Palenque. You will know it soon, we will go there."

"Did you ever meet an American guy named Frank?"

"Frank? No, why?"

I was glad she didn't know him. It meant that Victor's story about the snake handler was wrong. It was probably just a coincidence that her name was Eva. Surely Frank was alone. Somewhere.

"Popalotl," I repeated, trying to memorize the baby's new name. "She's drinking well today."

"I am glad she is a girl," Ana said. "I've heard of one young male who seized his trainer with his trunk, and stomped him to death."

Ana laughed, but there was a sadness to her. She tried again to put the nipple in Popalotl's little mouth. But the baby's eyes rolled up and closed.

Ana looked so very far away as she pulled a piece of tissue from her pocket and slowly wiped the milk from around the little elephant's mouth.

The circus trucks traveled in the night, leaving as soon as they could tear down the tents.

Everyone else was asleep, and didn't seem to notice when we pulled out. Josefa, the cook, was sprawled like an overstuffed doll on the bunk below mine, her deflated breasts falling off to each side, her two small children cuddled Pisces-style on the other bed.

I was still in my costume. The floor was dirty and my bunk was high, so I undressed standing up. The skirt and leotard that used to be Ana's smelled as rich as lion sweat.

I wanted to put my costume away, but I couldn't find the right drawer. It was dark, so I could feel, but I could barely see. The first drawer I opened was filled with clothing and odd things children play with -- rope and plastic bottles, a headless doll, a flattened ball.

I didn't intend to slam the drawer shut as loudly as it did. I startled, standing there naked, hoping I hadn't awakened the cook or her children.

The smallest child cried "¡Mama!" and thrashed about. I covered him with a sheet and stroked his head until he fell asleep. Then I climbed alone in my own bunk, stuck my costume under my pillow, and slept like I belonged there.

I couldn't tell how late it was when I woke up. Josefa and the kids were gone. The window in the trailer was covered with Josefa's shawl. Peeking through the long black fringe, I could see circus trucks and trailers and cages and vans and the old bus that was our kitchen. There were eleven vehicles in all, housing nineteen circus characters (including two children and myself) with tents and all the trappings.

I put on my jeans and went out to look for breakfast. We were parked in the middle of a wide empty street that ended in a cul-de-sac with a beautiful old cathedral. I could see poor Enrique working hard, helping to raise the tents in a field not far away.

Josefa stood at a table in front of the food bus. Her jiggly-soft arms were covered to the elbow with blood. In her hands was a large pig organ, like a donor heart waiting to be put inside a man who needed it. The pig lay in pieces on the table. She ripped apart the organ and threw the pieces into a pot of water while her children played hide and seek under her faded skirt.

"Es tarde para desayunar," said Josefa.

I had almost missed breakfast. There were two long skinny tables where everyone ate together. I filled a tortilla from a pot of beans and put some salsa on top. I wanted a big breakfast so I wouldn't have to eat Josefa's soup.

Curso sat down next me on the bench. We could see Ana, off under a tree, working with Lasse. They laughed together as he taught her how to throw knives at a stuffed dummy with a feathered hat that was mounted on a round target and tied to a tree.

"You sleep well?" Curso asked me. His smell was heavy and damp, like he'd been working hard already with the animals.

I nodded.

"Good hard work, fresh air, helps sleep, no?"

Curso squinted his eyes as he watched Lasse stand behind Ana and put his arms around her, adjusting her stance and the knife she held in her left hand. Lasse stood back as Ana aimed and threw the knife. It hit right beside the dummy's head. Lasse clapped and Ana tried again.

"A lucky accident," shouted Curso.

"No, no, she is getting good," said Lasse.

Ana smiled proudly at Curso. She threw again, but the knife missed the target entirely, disappearing into the brush behind the tree. Curso broke into a long deep laugh. Ana glared at him. They never really talked much. They just exchanged looks.

People think loudly sometimes. It wasn't Ana's mind that I could read, but her feelings, coming in as clearly as if they were my own. I knew, for instance, that when the Swede touched the Pink Lady's arm, she felt it all through her body. I don't know how, but I also knew that Ana had once had a baby and that something bad had happened. And that she had lost more love than I could ever dream of having.

I had no idea what town I was in, but I knew where Frank was. Since I hadn't found him in Mazatlán, he had to be in Chiapas, or at least on his way there. Mazatlán and Chiapas were the only two places he had talked about.

Now if I could only figure out where I was. Mexico was a much larger country than I had thought.

"¿Donde está el zócalo?" I asked a shop lady. I knew there would be other travelers in the zocalo, or town square.

The shop lady said the square was seven or eight blocks away, but I walked ten blocks and didn't find it. I asked again, this time in a bakery. The baker said three blocks to my left. But it wasn't there. I never did find it.

I saw a group of kids at a juice stand, so I stopped and ordered a manzana con leche. All the seats were taken and I stood on the sidewalk behind the people who seemed to know each other. I was tired of asking if anyone knew Frank, so I just eavesdropped, hoping to get a clue. But the kids drinking juice today spoke only German. They seemed to be comparing how dirty their jeans were and laughing.

The woman behind the stand kept her eye on me, making sure I did not run off with her glass. A German guy left and I was going to grab a seat, but a girl beat me to it. She had dirty blond hair and reminded me a little of Julia. Her boyfriend stood beside her. He had a beard and looked like a therapist. He reminded me of Julia's dad. Before I even heard them speak I knew they were from the States.

"Remember that lady yesterday? Asked if we'd seen a redhead?" the girl said to her boyfriend. She motioned toward me and I wasn't sure if I was supposed to pretend I didn't hear or what. "She described her perfectly. Red-hair, blue eyes, blue felt hat, cowboy boots."

"Yeah, could've been you." The guy smiled at me, flirtatiously.

"Wasn't me. I'm traveling alone. On business," I said. "But I'm looking for someone, too. An American guy named Frank. You wouldn't know him, would you?"

The girl answered. "He's a poet. Right? Name's Frank, but calls himself Pancho."

"No, no, no, no, no," said the bearded guy. "His name is Pancho, he calls himself Frank. He's Mexican."

"No, he just has a Mexican girlfriend."

"His girlfriend called him Frank. He played in a Goddamned mariachi band; he was no poet and he wasn't from the States."

They were starting to argue, and it wasn't about my Frank.

"Where are we, anyway?" I asked, but the girl ignored me. They were locked into their argument.

"He wasn't in a band. He was just eccentric," she said.

"Why would anyone wear an outfit that uncomfortable for fun?"

"Excuse me, what town is this?" I interrupted. "Are we north or south of Mazatlán?"

"South," the girl said. "We're just east of Guadalajara."

"We're not east of Guadalajara," said the guy. "We're directly below it. We're not east at all."

I finished my juice and set my glass on the counter. The woman behind the stand relaxed.

At least we were heading south. I could be sure that in a few weeks, when the eclipse took place, we would be somewhere near Chiapas.

Josefa's night job was as a clown. She circled the ring in a goose costume and her children, dressed as a frog and a duck, ran after her. She threw sparkling confetti at the audience, and always snatched another child or two from the front row, to follow her once around the ring before her exit.

Families with more than five kids got a discount. I could see the clowns and the big crowd from the wings. Hundreds of balloons filled the rafters. Two new klieg lights swept stripes of red and purple across the big top.

I entered as the band played the post-intermission song, a strange version of reveille. I placed a red blanket on the ground in front of the Plymouth, which was parked inside the ring. I extended my arm in a gesture that welcomed Curso with great flair. The drums rolled and a couple of horns blew proudly out of tune.

Curso ran in smiling, arms raised to receive the slight applause. He wore gold lamé pants and matching knee-high boots with a fingernail moon on his right boot and a black star on his left. His black leather gloves came to a point at his elbows and were also decorated with stars and moons.

I stood there awkwardly, my hands on my hips and my legs in

the charm school pose my mother had taught me when I was five. I couldn't remember if I was supposed to run off stage or stay.

Curso lay on his back on the blanket with his feet under the front of the Plymouth. The palms of his gloves and the soles of his boots were deeply worn. Sweat wet his face as he raised his legs and pushed upwards against the underside of the car. The Plymouth rose slightly, as the audience counted in unison. Curso grunted with fierce strength, as if he were Atlas holding up the world. *¡Dieciocho, diecinueve, veinte!* Curso raised the car another few inches. He suddenly dropped it and jumped up, bowing his head while horns blasted. I ran behind him as he left.

The applause was weak. The next act ran on immediately. Ana entered the ring wearing a headdress of pink feathers and was followed by Lasse juggling hatchets. I watched from the wings as Ana spread her arms and legs in front of the bright red target and replaced the bull's-eye with her body. The Swede picked up a belt full of knives and buckled it around his hips. He took a stance twenty feet in front of Ana and pulled out a knife, moving the large blade so it caught the light.

There was silence as Lasse threw the first knife. It landed an inch from Ana's foot. The audience seemed hypnotized as the tall blond threw twenty knives, one by one. Every blade landed with a loud thud, until Ana was totally surrounded. I'd forgotten to breathe and felt dizzy as I watched Lasse take his bow. The audience applauded furiously.

Pacing in the wings, Curso licked his mustache and cracked his knuckles. The crowd stood and yelled and stomped and clapped until Lasse returned for several more bows.

The clowns were quibbling backstage. One had dropped his pants in the middle of another's pie throw. "¿Cual es el problema?" Josefa asked, trying to mediate.

Curso suddenly turned to me, his eyes like piercing arrows. "Come on. New act. You do exactly as Ana did in rehearsal."

"What, the lions?"

"No, no, something new."

"But...."

"It easy, it's easy. I do the work. ¡Ándale, ándale!" He pushed me into the ring. Behind me, Curso led Enrique to center stage. I stood there feeling foolish. I had no idea what was next.

Enrique knelt down. Using the elephant's knee as a stair, Curso climbed up onto his back.

"Come," he whispered, and held out a hand.

I could reach Curso's hand only by climbing the elephant stair. I let Curso pull me up. He was right, it was incredibly easy. I got my balance on Enrique's back, and quickly learned to sway with his twitching muscles. I fully trusted Enrique not to make any sudden moves. I was finally standing on top of an elephant.

We circled the ring and then stopped close to the front row.

"Find a face you like in the audience and don't take your eyes from it," Curso whispered. There was a young boy in the front row, eight or nine, staring with anticipation. I tried to smile at him and felt my lips shake. The boy didn't smile back.

"Backup!" Curso grunted and, keeping my arms spread for balance, I inched back on the huge beast toward Curso. "Now, SIT." I started to sit down on the elephant but Curso's voice was furious, threatening. "MY HAND, NIÑA, RIGHT HERE, MY HAND!"

I did as I was told and his hand cradled my crotch as he swept me up into the air, high above Enrique, too high above the ground. The little boy and the crowd became a blur of pink and purple.

I held my breath and tried to balance my body, but couldn't. I was shaking as Curso lowered me to Enrique's back.

"We try again," he said, impatiently, in a shouted whisper. "You try harder."

He put his hand between my legs again, this time slipping it under my leotard. "Better grip," he grinned.

I tried to smile at the audience, as I had seen Ana do. But I was so dizzy I couldn't see. I looked for something outside of myself to focus on, like a ballet teacher had once taught me. But nothing would stand still, except Curso's jet-black hair below me, gleaming in the purple light.

Two huge fingers sank deep between the cheeks of my butt, as his thumb grasped my crotch. I swayed a bit and then regained my balance.

Below him, the elephant's back muscles swayed like ocean waves and far beneath that was the ground, hard and unforgiving. I pictured myself, splattered, broken bones and pools of blood. I wondered how far a human could fall without facing instant death.

I tried to sleep that night, while the truck rocked back and forth on good roads and bounced up and down on bad. I wondered how the baby elephant was taking the ride, and thought about how demanding show business was, and how hard it must be to be born into it. Movies, circus, it was all so much alike. Make-up, costumes, trailers, lights, sex, blood, and drama. And snakes.

A bright green lizard with only half a tail walked upside down on the ceiling above my bunk. My head was killing me, my butt was bruised, and I had mosquito bites all over my face and legs. Big swollen pink welts, like the ones I always used to get while fishing at Grandma's.

Grandma thought she had a fish, I remember once, but when she got her line untangled and pulled it up, all that was on it was a snapping turtle.

"Dog-goned nasty old turtle ate my bait," she said. She cut the turtle's head off and threw her line back in. We settled down again to wait for a catfish.

"Mom kicked Dad out," I said.

"Yeah, I was afeared of that." She put her arm around me and we watched the red balls float in the pond.

"When your Daddy was growing up we didn't partake in the

things of this world. Then he moved out to Californy and got mixed up with that Hollywood bunch."

The turtle walked around in the mud with a bloody stump where his head used to be. He acted like he didn't know he was missing something.

Chickens flop around after they've had their heads wrung off. This lizard walked on the ceiling without his tail. But a lizard can grow a new tail. I'd never heard of anyone growing a new head.

11

Knives

A WROUGHT IRON CHANDELIER HUNG twenty feet overhead
in the entry of the old colonial home. Bright red carpet ran up the
staircase, as far as I could see. I was the only person in the circus invited to stay with Ana and Curso at his mother's house in Morelia, in
the mountains of central Mexico.

An elderly servant showed me to a guest room with a big wooden
bed. She gave me towels and put a chocolate on my pillow. It was all
so formal. I felt disoriented and out of place. I went into the bathroom and checked the medicine cabinet, hoping to find a tranquilizer
or a pain pill to help me check out.

There was nothing there besides a tube of toothpaste and a jar of
Vaseline. I closed the door to the medicine cabinet. Curso appeared
in the mirror behind me. I was startled.

"I was looking for this, for my lips," I said, getting the Vaseline out of the cabinet. "The mountain air made them dry."

"Mine too," he said.

I opened the jar and spread some jelly on my lips. There was still some left on my finger, so naturally, I reached over to spread it on Curso's cracked lips. I mean, we were living like family.

But Curso grabbed my wrist. "Don't do that," he said firmly, staring into my eyes as if to make a point, before he abruptly dropped my arm. He closed the door behind him as he left.

I undressed and turned on the shower. The water felt like it was getting warm. I hadn't taken a hot shower in weeks. Traveling with the circus was rough. I wondered how many towns I'd have to visit before I'd find Frank.

Somewhere, I'd be performing and a man in the front row would move, and behind him, I'd see Frank's dark wondrous eyes. I'd climb down from Enrique, entranced. Frank would ignore the woman he was with and our eyes would lock, too intensely to allow us even to smile. He'd get up and walk toward me in slow motion, like Jesus on water, and the audience would fade away, as we fell into a kiss.

I couldn't help but release guttural moans, as the gloriously hot water rushed down my back.

When I opened the door of the bathroom, Curso was standing in the hall, as if waiting for something. I had a big white towel wrapped around me and my skin was steaming. I ran past him and into my room.

The tile floor was cold, there was no heat, only a fireplace without wood. There was a trunk with many drawers, and a table covered with an old delicately sewn rebozo. A picture of a woman dressed in leaves hung on the wall above the table where you might expect a mirror. She wore pearls around her waist and roses around her neck.

I got under the thick down quilt. Everything was so clean. I unwrapped the chocolate and let it dissolve in my mouth.

Church bells rang all night and I could barely sleep. I counted the rings but they made no sense. Six rings and ten minutes later only two.

I stared up into the dark and touched the soft part of my ear. My body was strangely alert. I pictured Frank with a young traveler, her long black hair covering his face as he lay below, licking her breasts, so much larger and fuller than mine. I put my hand inside my panties and as I did, I saw Frank so clearly, making love with his dark stranger, that it almost felt real. He kissed her neck, which at that moment was mine, long as an Egyptian queen, skin dark and smooth. He came so close I could smell his warm neck and then he whispered "Will you have my baby?" and it meant that he wanted to love me forever, and I said yes, yes, yes, and we sank deeply into the white feather bed and we both said yes again.

Later I hoped no sounds had come out of me. Afterwards, I wanted to be held.

Ana and Lasse rehearsed in a large empty lot on the edge of town, while the workers pitched the tents nearby. Curso and I returned from the market with a truckload of mystery meat.

The circus was in trouble and Curso was complaining. Several large cities, including Guadalajara, had already canceled, and he was afraid that Mexico City might follow suit. The tour, which normally ran for six months straight, from home base in Morelia to the northern beaches where I had joined them, down to Cuernavaca and the silver country, and then further south through Chiapas, now zigzagged all over the place, with big holes in the schedule, often for days at a time. Curso had managed to book two weekends in his hometown, Morelia, but in-between was unwanted downtime.

"El mundo cambio!" Curso moaned, as he hoisted a huge bag of scrap meat out of the bed of the truck. "The cities get bigger and my circus gets smaller," he muttered. He grabbed a greasy rag from the back of the pick-up as Ana and Lasse rode past, practicing on top of Enrique.

Ana sat on the Swede's broad shoulders, her legs tucked under his biceps. Her arms were up in the air, hands open to the sky. She was smiling gloriously.

Curso's brow crinkled and he wiped his bloody hands on the rag.

"Enough already! I have ideas." He threw the rag back into the truck, resolutely. "I have a new job for you," he said to me, gleaming. "Come!"

He dragged the heavy bag of meat toward the hungry lions. He opened the gate of a large lioness' cage and went in, closing the gate behind him. The golden animal rose to her feet. Curso held out a hunk of dripping red meat and then dumped it on the floor. The lioness immediately grabbed it, retreated to a corner of her cage, placed it between her paws, and went to ripping it apart. Her purr rumbled like an earthquake, as she worked herself into a feeding frenzy.

Curso stepped down from the cage. "Today you watch. Tomorrow, you feed her. That's how you will make friends."

"Who said I need friends?"

He laughed. "You don't know your own fire, do you? If she likes you, we can do a wonderful act."

Curso tossed meat to the next lion. He paused to watch as Enrique stopped nearby. Ana and Lasse slid from the elephant, talking loudly and playfully. They didn't seem to notice us.

Curso slammed the door to the cage and stomped towards Lasse.

"We don't need you anymore," he declared.

Everyone became silent.

"¿Qué?" said Lasse, taken aback.

"No necisito tu trabajo." Curso grinned and nodded his head back toward me. "Better two women and one man, than one woman and two men, no?"

Lasse looked puzzled.

"You're cutting Lasse from the elephant act?" asked Ana.

"Why not? I'll cut knives, too. I have a new act, even sexier. Lions and a beautiful girl."

Ana shook her head in disbelief.

Curso smiled and purred at her, deep in his throat, just like the lioness: "Nothing is more beautiful than a young woman with a cat."

"Pinche pendejo," Lasse said, which means something like stupid ass. He shook his head furiously as he stormed off toward his trailer.

"I'm going to bathe Lola," Ana said.

"You're not finished rehearsing," Curso growled.

"No?" Ana said. She walked away.

"You should marry that stubborn elephant," Curso shouted, his finger raised and shaking, his face burning red.

Ana's gaze rested on the dust of Lasse's wake. She smiled sadly, with only her eyes.

I followed Ana as she led Lola beyond the camp where the trailers were parked and down a dirt road, past many narrow paths and muddy ditches. I listened hard to the music of the birds, and to the lumbering clump of Lola's heavy feet. Ana was silent. I didn't mention that it was my birthday.

My feet were dirty and I liked that, the dirt covered their stark whiteness and made them seem hearty and strong.

We entered a forested area, a lush tropical mix of trees that didn't look like they belonged together. Gigantic dark-green leaves, tiny yellow-green ferns, so many colors, all called green. Palms above us reached to the sky, each balancing on its skinny trunk, like an ostrich on one leg. I sank gently into the soggy ground, mud seeping up over my thongs. I could hear the river before I saw it. A group of women were gathered on the other side, upstream, washing clothes. An occasional Dos Equis bottle and several white plastic bleach bottles were scattered on the bank. The sky was cloudy and the river looked murky.

Ana pulled a handful of carrots out of a burlap bag and fed them to Lola, who backed her hind feet into the muddy water.

"You have good balance," Ana said.

"Not really," I shrugged, looking at Lola's thick wrinkled knees.

Ana handed me an apple. Lola grabbed it, using the tip of her trunk as a hand. "You must be careful with Enrique. That trunk can grasp as well as our thumb and forefinger. His grip is stronger than you can imagine."

"Enrique would never hurt me."

"I see you care for him. But love him with open eyes. He may be friendly, but he is still an animal. Vamos al agua. Lola necesita un baño."

We took our clothes off and hung them on a branch. Ana's naked body wasn't pin-up pretty, her breasts were small and low. But she held her head high and proud. Her soft black mustache glistened with sweat. I always hated a woman's mustache, but on Ana it looked beautiful, perfect with her deep black eyes and braided pink hair, wrapped around her head in graceful curls. I wondered how she did her hair that way. There were no pins or clips that I could see.

We waded in, pulling Lola behind us. I tried wrapping my own hair up like Ana's, so it wouldn't get wet. But my breasts felt too exposed, and my hair wouldn't stay up anyway.

Ana carried a bucket with a rag and soap. She told Lola to kneel and we washed her as far as we could reach. Then Lola got up suddenly, knocking us both down. We fell together and laughed while Lola stomped her feet and splashed us both.

"How does your hair stay up without bobby pins?" I asked Ana when the laughter died.

She smiled a gentle laugh. "What makes you think I don't use bobby pins?"

"I don't know. I couldn't see them."

"Then I've made magic!" Ana laughed and slapped Lola on the

butt. Together, we got out of the muddy water and put clothes on our wet bodies.

"Are you in love with Lasse?" I asked.

Ana pulled her cotton sweater over her head. "I don't fall in love anymore," she said. "I was once so in love that I ruined someone's life. Now I love only my work."

Ana's laugh reminded me of my own, a laughter that covered a broken heart.

"What happened?"

"He made me choose, between him and my baby girl. I made the wrong choice."

"Where's your daughter?"

"In another world," Ana said. "Alive, but in another world."

For the first time in weeks, I thought about home, and the story my mom used to tell me on my birthdays. "I'm the one who should be celebrating," she always said. And then she'd tell me about when she was sixteen and frightened, and how the day I was born the pain was so bad she wanted to die. I wanted to hear her tell it again.

Ana moved a strand of hair that hung over my eyes and tucked it behind my ears. She didn't say, "Would you get that God-damned hair out of your eyes, it's driving me crazy." She just ran one finger gently over my ear and down my neck. I wanted to cry.

"How come you're so nice to me?" I asked.

"What a funny question!" Ana pulled the sleeve up on her sweater. "Don't ever hate the other woman," she said. "It's never her fault."

Curso's mother wore a deep red silk blouse and her black braids were wrapped neatly around her head. She stared straight ahead while a servant spooned black sauce over the chicken on her plate. Behind her, on the dining room wall, hung a painting, a scene in some provincial kitchen, done with dark browns and deep reds. Game birds with broken necks lay on an old wooden table next to a dead rabbit, sprawled out on his back with his legs spread open. The rabbit's stomach looked soft and vulnerable, like it had already been skinned.

I sat across the immense table from Ana, who looked slightly down at her plate and didn't speak.

It had been so long since I'd put a napkin in my lap, I was uncomfortable trying to be civilized. Curso's foot reached deep under the table and leaned on mine. It was lively enough to let me know he didn't think mine was a table's leg. I drank the heavy red wine in huge gulps and a servant filled my glass.

"¿Qué hace su padre?" The old lady wanted to know. The skin on the hand she used to lift her knife looked like a roasted chicken, dry, red, and crinkled.

"And what does your father do?" Curso translated for her.

"He's a lawyer."

"Un abogado," Curso told her.

She nodded in approval. "Mi hijo está en el Circo. Es un 'rebel without a cause.' Por eso, no tengo nietos." She looked at Ana.

"She said because her son's a rebel, she has no grandson." Ana told me. "She means the circus and me. We were both below his class."

"Maybe we will have this grandson yet," Curso grinned.

Ana took a deep breath and smiled. "When I was small I dreamed of flying airplanes, as my father did," she said. She spoke sweetly to me, as if we were alone. "My mother said yes when you are big, you will fly. Then I fell in love with Curso. We flew the trapeze. Now I'm getting old."

"You're not old, Ana," I said. I'd never thought of her as old, I thought she was epitome of womanhood, incredibly beautiful and wise. She knew how to live.

Ana smiled and blessed me with soft-focused eyes. "You're young, you still think time is endless."

"Nothing's endless," I said. "Everything ends."

La Señora de León rang a small silver bell to call the servant, maybe, or simply to bring our attention back to her. "¿No tienes un novio?" she asked me.

"She's asking if you have a boyfriend," Ana said.

"I have a boyfriend. But I don't know where he is." I hoped she didn't understand. "I'll find him," I said. "That's why I'm here."

"If he wanted to be with you, he would find you," Ana said.

"Quiere más vino?" said the old lady, taking a sip of red wine. Her arms were covered with puffy veins and blue splotches.

"Would you care for more wine?" said Curso, as the servant poured some into his glass.

I licked my lips and let my glass be filled and drank it down.

I was lying in bed in a fitful half-sleep, wishing I hadn't drunk so much. My jaw ached with tension and worry. Maybe Frank didn't want me. It had been months now, since we had been together. Maybe he did run off with a snake handler, or maybe he went back to his old girlfriend, Eva. Or maybe he just plain didn't want me.

On the other hand, Ana didn't know anything. I'd gotten way too involved with her. Why was I even listening to what she had to say? This circus job was only meant to be temporary, to make some money, travel, and find Frank. I'd saved the equivalent of a hundred dollars. It was time to leave. Everything ends in time. Time is only endless in our dreams.

I dreamed I ran with fireflies and heard crickets singing age-old gospel in the rotting wooden house where my grandmother grew up. Just like I had in real life, I opened the dusty old trunk that Grandma always told me not to mess with. Inside I found wasps nests on an old wool coat, wire rim glasses and a pair of gold earrings, a piece of squirrel fur, a small handcrafted knife, a box of arrowheads. I unwrapped a yellowed pillowcase and held in my hands two long black braids, cut from my great-grandma's head.

I was barely awake as he lifted the sheet, and crawled in next to me. I hadn't heard him come in, but the moment his naked body eased down onto mine, I knew I'd been dreaming of it all along.

El Gran Curso covered my mouth gently. "Shhh... we make a present," he smiled. My next breath took in his damp rich smell.

He relaxed weight of his furry chest onto my breast, and I was surprised by my own trembling sigh.

He spoke in a low growl of the Pink Lady, even as he put his fingers in my private hair, rubbing softly as he whispered in my ear.

"We can't do this," I said, knowing it was going to happen anyway.

"It's good, it is okay with her."

I felt his breath on my ear, loud and damp as a lion's. Life was crazy and I was game and frightened and excited and soft and wet and warm. He entered me in one deep hungry thrust and I felt vicious and brightly alive. For a moment I was endless and powerful, and as beautiful as Ana.

But in the night, after he had gone, the world got dark. The tree outside the bedroom window was brown and leafless, with long thin limbs that wrapped around themselves like a knotty witch's hand.

I started to sweat, and the bed sheets felt like a dark mossy lake, and I noticed that the walls peeled around the edges like a moldy clay pot.

I wondered if I'd slept or not. Twelve church bells and it must have been five in the morning. It was getting light. I was afraid to move, and grew more and more miserable as the dawn went on, feeling as if I was evolving backwards into a wet newborn, and then splitting into sperm and egg in my teenage mother's womb.

The old servant poured hot coffee and steaming milk. I drank it down quickly even though it burnt my mouth.

"Donde está Ana?" Curso's mother asked as she nodded to the servant to place bread upon the plate in front of Ana's empty chair.

"Está enojada," Curso answered. He finished his explanation with a teasing smile, for my sake. "I stopped by her room. She is still angry because I have an act with a lion and girl, and won't permit Ana's knives."

La Señora de León seemed to understand her son's English. The look on her face was purposeful and knowing, as if to say I told you so.

Ana walked in and politely greeted everyone. She sat down and began to butter her bread. I could see in her face that she knew, and that it wasn't at all okay with her.

The room seemed to grow smaller. I drank a second cup of coffee. I looked to see if there was a window to open.

Curso's mother held out a gift wrapped in red velvet with a gold ribbon. "Ana?" she said. Ana rose to receive it, then returned to her seat, setting the present beside her plate. She began quietly eating bread.

"No va a abrirlo?" The old lady spoke quite formally.

"Cómo no." Ana dutifully untied the ribbon and unwrapped the present.

Ana's box contained a necklace, emerald and silver, like something a queen might wear. She politely got up and kissed La Señora de León on each cheek. Then she sat back down and placed the necklace on her neck, over her pink satin robe, and let it lay there, unfastened, for us all to admire.

La Señora de León reached out her long velvet covered arm and handed me a small gift. I stared at the veins in her old leather hands. My own hand was shaky as I took the package and wondered why there was a gift for me.

"It's just a token. Is not the circus one big family?" the old lady said in English. "I don't mean to annoy my daughter-in-law."

La Señora de León looked at me, standing over my plate with the gift in my hand. I shuddered, repelled. I didn't want the present. I wanted to run out of the room and out the door, but nothing seemed to exist except the tiny space I sat in and the strange red box I was opening and the ruby teardrop earrings I found inside.

When I went to kiss La Señora de León, as Ana had done, La Señora took my hand in hers. Her perfume mixed with fresh bread, and I was sure it covered a smell of something rotting.

Ana stayed in her room that day, until late afternoon, when I heard her in the courtyard. From my window, I saw she was alone, practicing with the knives. I watched as she surrounded the dummy, her weapons zipping through the air, one by one, landing with a sharp thump. She looked angry, and determined not to let it get her down. She seemed more focused now than ever. She never missed.

Curso entered silently, leaned on the wooden horse that adorned the courtyard, and watched. I remembered pictures of Renaissance statues with tiny penises, smaller than thumbs, so out of proportion. But this huge wooden horse that stood in the courtyard of Curso's mother had the opposite problem. His penis was thicker than his thighs, almost as wide as Curso's muscular body.

As Ana pulled her knives from the target, she noticed her husband standing there.

"I'm ready to perform this act," she said very deliberately. "Since you insist on firing Lasse, at least let me have the act."

Curso laughed and then froze in a grin until Ana's silent glare made him shift position.

"Who would be your target?"

"You," she said.

Curso broke into an even louder laugh. Ana turned her back and headed to the door. Reaching the steps, she turned toward Curso and threw a knife onto the ground. It landed in the grout between two stone tiles, to the left of Curso's foot.

She smiled to see him jump. Then, noticing me, she said, "Our young friend would make a lovely target. And my costumes fit."

Curso threw back his head, laughing with great pleasure. "Why not?"

"Sure, why not?" I said. "I'll pose for the knives."

Curso laughed even louder. He took me by the arm and placed me a few feet in front of Ana. "Let me see," he said.

He backed up and looked through a frame he made with his hands.

"Increblé," he said. "Like a movie poster."

He walked up to Ana and put his arm proudly around her shoulder.

"My wife. She is really something."

I planned to sleep in my trailer, if I could find where the circus was parked. I remembered it was near a park called El Estribo, in a big empty lot. I asked a construction worker where El Estribo was. He said it was seven blocks north.

I walked up several blocks of cobbled road overlooking the city of Morelia, all the way past the cathedral to the lake with five islands. I turned off the main road and walked in and out of a residential area, past bright pink and turquoise homes with open windows. I could see the people inside as I passed, watching TV or sitting down to eat. But I still hadn't found El Estribo. A child who was selling gum said it was four blocks to the east, running parallel to the street I'd been walking on, so I went that way. I stopped counting after several minutes. I had ended up back in the main part of town. I was totally lost.

I looked around for someone to ask. I was in front of city hall and the jail. The bars of the jail were just above the ground and I could see eyes peeking out at my ankles. It gave me the creeps so I backed off, only to find myself in front of an open coffin.

It was displayed on the sidewalk, next to a sign that said BARATO – cheap. A mannequin dressed in a bridal gown lay in the pink velvet lining of the coffin. The metal was as thick and shiny as a fire truck.

"Hey, is your name Sean?" a voice asked.

An Asian girl with huge moon and star earrings was walking toward me. She was with a dark-skinned boy and they both looked very exotic, like they'd been living on a Caribbean island.

She acted like she might know me, and it scared me a bit, because I'd never seen her before in my life.

"Why?"

"Someone was looking for a redhead named Sean." She turned to her boyfriend. "Who was that?"

"Was it a guy? Frank?" I said, almost flying out of my clothes.

"No, it was a woman."

"Oh." It seemed like it suddenly got dark and I was as lost as I'd ever been. "No it's not me. Nobody knows me around here, except the people I work with. Hey, do you know where El Estribo is?"

The man spoke with a French accent. "What are you looking for?"

"The circus."

The guy took me by the shoulder and led me about six blocks back up the hill to an empty parking lot.

"Right there," he said, and pointed up the block at the familiar colored tents.

Josefa knelt before a small altar she'd made, in the corner of our trailer, out of plastic flowers and melted wax and a statue of the Virgin Mary. There was a plate of burnt tortillas and bread baked in the shape of a rabbit.

I had never seen Josefa so still. She was always cooking, cleaning, chasing kids, making others laugh. She looked warmly toward me, but did not smile as she moved to make room at the altar.

It was good to be back home in my trailer. Kneeling on the worn cushion, I thought of how much more civilized Catholics were than Baptists like my grandparents, who knelt on the cold hard floor. Josefa lit a candle and placed it on the altar between a pair of baby shoes and a doll dressed in dirty lace.

I stared at the candle and wondered how close we were to Chiapas. The eclipse would be very soon. I lit a candle for Frank. It was a lovely thing to do. Flickering fire and a wish.

Josefa stood up abruptly and looked down at me, her hands on her hips. In a voice too harsh and loud for the solemnity of the occasion, she said: "¡El elefante se murió!"

"The baby died?"

"Sí. No comió nada," she said.

The baby elephant never ate and now she was dead. I wondered if there wasn't something we could have done to save her. Maybe I should have tried to feed her candy bars or Pepsi, food my teen-aged mother fed me. Now the baby was dead and even mother's milk would not revive her.

Josefa lay down on the cot, next to her sleeping children. She almost immediately began to snore.

From my bunk, I stared out the window, listening to the sounds of people cleaning up the grounds.

It was dark outside, but there was movement. I noticed something unusual in back of the trailer beside mine. I leaned on my elbow to take a closer look.

The phantom moved and I realized it was two people embracing. They held one another for a long time before their shadows separated.

A cage door slammed and a lion roared. The generator shut down and the lights went out. I wished I had someone to talk to.

At dawn, the trucks stood by, all packed and ready to go to Palenque. Ana had a pink tiara in her hands, and I held real flowers. We had planned a funeral for Popalotl. A deep hole had been dug in the empty lot. Lola stood over her baby's lifeless body. I wondered how long it took to dig an elephant grave.

Curso returned from his walk with Enrique. He walked the elephant every morning, and if he missed, Enrique would refuse to perform. But today, a walk was not enough to cheer the male elephant. The dark streaks that ran down Enrique's face, so that he always looked like he had just finished crying, were even darker, and in fact looked wet.

Enrique stopped just short of the truck, ignoring Curso's directions to step up onto the ramp. The elephant looked back at Lola and watched as Lola, with her trunk, examined her baby's mouth, under the ear, the circles around her sweet tiny eyes. Lola's touch was tender. Not like a mother who had let her child die. It was a lullaby, a kiss goodnight.

Two workmen approached the dead baby, intending to push the body toward the hole. The moment they got within an arm's length, Lola raised her trunk to the sky with a trumpet blast. She reared up onto her hind legs, threatening to land on anyone who dared to touch her offspring.

Enrique pulled away from Curso and walked toward Lola. She calmed down as she saw him coming. She reached out to him; their trunks intertwined in an elephant embrace.

Curso grabbed a stick and went after Enrique.

"¡Vámanos!"

Enrique flapped his trunk, slapping Curso on the backside. Curso hit Enrique again.

"Stop it!" I yelled. For a moment I thought Curso was going to hit me, so I backed off. I didn't know what it felt like to be hit by a stick, but I knew being whipped by my daddy's belt was bad enough.

Curso hit him yet again. "¡Pinche Elefantes!"

My eyes caught Ana's. I could see that she wanted to stop him. But she looked at the ground instead, biting the inside of her cheek.

"Don't you hate him?" I said. It was safer than asking if she hated me.

"You must work with what you have," Ana said. She wore a slight, ironic smile. "We are all many people."

"¡Vámanos, come!" Curso shouted at the drivers and then at the rest of us. Enrique had finally stepped into his truck and now Curso was guiding Lola.

The little ceremony we had planned would not take place. The baby would not be buried. It was time to go.

Ana squinted as she looked at Curso. "Soon I will retire from trapeze. Maybe even from marriage, take my knife act on the road!" Ana laughed and seemed to relish her fantasy. For a moment she reminded me of my mother. Her gaiety, so far from the grief she really felt, like wine poured on a broken heart.

Josefa covered the baby with a woven shawl and Ana placed the pink tiara on the side of her head. I put my flowers at her feet. A part of me wanted to leave my blue hat. But she didn't need a hat. She was on her way to heaven in a tiara.

As we pulled away, I watched big black birds land on Popalotl. Her body would at least be useful in death. Perhaps flowers or grain would grow in that fertile place, after she turned to minerals and dust.

At least she wasn't going to be buried in a fancy steel casket. I have always been afraid of metal caskets. Frank once told me they stop your soul.

Maybe that's what is wrong with the world. All the souls that should be guiding us were buried airtight in thick steel and have never gotten free.

12

The Escape

IT WAS EVENING WHEN WE turned down a dirt road, into a
thick dark jungle. Curso and Ana were behind us in the elephant
truck, followed by more trucks, the lion cages, vans, and the old blue
van that the musicians slept in. We were down to nine vehicles in all,
since we'd lost Lasse as a driver.

We pulled into a clearing where a cluster of metal-roofed rectan-
gles gathered around a muddy yard, alive with chickens, turkeys, and
pigs. A very old woman stood over a concrete sink, washing a large
glass jar. She squinted in our direction, but didn't seem to see us. A
naked toddler stared at us for a moment and then disappeared into a
doorway, returning with a dozen pair of small dark eyes.

Ana jumped out of the other truck. By the time her feet hit
the ground, three excited children were leading her toward the old

woman, who was still hunched over the sink. As she slowly recognized Ana, the old lady wiped her hands on her apron and a peaceful smile lit up her face.

Ana hugged her grandmother and introduced me. The old lady searched my face with her clouded eyes and shook my hand in both of hers. I wondered how much of me she could see.

I suddenly heard Enrique bang back and forth in his cage, ten thousand pounds of bull elephant. Ana returned to the truck to see what was going on. I followed close behind.

Curso had unloaded Lola and was driving her stake into the ground, several yards from the truck. She flapped her torn ears and paced the length of her chain. Curso cursed.

Ana stood in front of Enrique's cage. She pulled me back when I got less than a trunk's distance from the bars. Enrique had a truly wild look in his eyes, and a dark secretion seeped from the thick skin above his eyelid.

"What is it?" I asked.

Ana spoke only to her husband. She whispered. Curso clenched his teeth and shook his head.

"It is his time," Ana said emphatically.

"No problema," Curso said. He went to open the cage.

Enrique swung his trunk impatiently.

"Don't do it," Ana said, shaking her head nervously.

"Why not? Pobre Enrique. He wants out of the cage. I'm tired of the truck, too."

Curso opened the cage and let Enrique step down.

Enrique blew his horn, as if calling wild girl elephants down from the heavens.

He threw his huge head back and his front legs rose suddenly in the air, knocking Curso down hard onto the ground. Curso quickly scampered out of the elephant's way.

"What did I tell you?" Ana yelled. "He's of age; he's in his danger time. Can't you smell it?"

Curso cowered for a moment. Then he brushed himself off, stood straight up and stuck his chest out.

"Nonsense, no problem," he said gruffly. "We'll chain him up, until the show tonight."

"He can't perform," Ana said. "¿Estás loco?"

"No, you are the crazy one. A circus with just one elephant? What kind of world is that?"

The circus trucks were parked in a half-circle with plants up to the top of their wheels. I wondered if by morning our trucks might be covered in jungle. Enrique seemed calm in his chains, which were threaded through the rotting holes in a corner of the old wooden barn.

Piglets ran around my feet as I entered the muddy courtyard. I bent down to pick one up, but it scurried away and disappeared into a dark living room. I could see the back of a couch with a sleeping man's head and feet sticking out either side. A television played with the sound off. It was a close-up of a young girl with thick eye make-up and huge red lips, who seemed to be mouthing a lost love ballad.

Ana's grandmother waved her hand toward her mouth asking if I had eaten. "No, gracias," I said. "Tengo hambre." She smiled a toothless smile and slapped me lovingly on the cheek. Then she lifted a rag off a plate of beans and heated a tortilla for me. Tired from the long drive, most of the circus people had gone to bed. I ate alone while Ana's grandmother sat quietly, looking down at her lap and rocking gently, as if in a pleasant dream.

When I was finished, she took me by the hand into a cool dark room. I could barely make out the contents: two metal cots across from each other against opposite walls, and an old double mattress on the floor near the third wall. I would have preferred the trailer, but Ana's grandmother had insisted we share her home. She took me to one of the cots and satisfied that I should rest there, she left.

The bed and the other cot were filled with human shadows. I

didn't know whose they were. Small animals walked slowly across the room. I hoped they weren't rats.

I lay down, fully clothed. My cot wasn't comfortable and the window was just a square hole with no glass or screen, so bugs came and went as they pleased. The rat turned out to be a small pig; two tiny babies scrambled after her. A mosquito buzzed in my ear. By morning I would be covered in big red welts, part of the hazard of being a thin-skinned redhead.

When I awoke, I could just make out the figures on the other beds. In the corner opposite my cot was Josefa, snoring with her children. Between us on the mattress, Ana and Curso moved quietly. I could have sworn that in the dawn and under the sheet, they made love.

I don't know if there are owls in Mexico, but there was a sound I heard at dawn that was both frightening and soothing. *Who – who -* telling me life was both mysterious and stark, and calling me farther south.

As soon as it was light, I slipped out. The old woman was already busy outside, patting tortillas. Two barefoot children giggled and pulled at my hands and circled me as I walked, until it wasn't clear if they followed me, or if I was following them.

The jungle around us was so alive it seemed to vibrate, but many of the buildings looked empty. Thick green vines climbed up walls and across boarded up doors and through broken windows. The packed dirt road was paved with pieces of colored bottle and old bottle caps that had been stepped on until they had become part of the path.

We stopped at a small store. Socks for sale were hung on top of the doorway, in rows from wire hangers. An Indian woman sat on the ground, leaning against the outside wall, and fed her infant brown liquid through a nipple especially made for the Coca-Cola bottle it was attached to.

A man stood at the counter buying cigarettes. He had sandy colored hair and looked like an old surfer. A bird was perched on his shoulder, yellow with a black head. Its squawk was loud and constant.

I searched through the dusty rows of baby food and packages of cigarettes and found a warm soda and a package of Chicharrones, Ana's favorite -- artificial pig rinds packaged like potato chips. I bought candy and gum for the children, and they ran away with it, laughing.

I wanted fresh yogurt and sweet mango, but when I touched and smelled the mango a woman shouted from behind the counter. "No tocar!!!"

"How the hell am I supposed to know if it's ripe or not!" I screamed in English.

The man with the bird laughed at me. "Can't try it until you buy it," he said. His skin was sun-worn with lines so deep his face looked scarred.

I followed him outside. "How far is Chiapas?"

"You're with the circus, aren't you?"

"Maybe."

"Just saw a guy nailing up a poster. I'm opposed."

"To what?"

"The circus. I don't believe in it. Can't tame a wild animal. Anyone who tries is out of their mind."

"It is an art."

"It's offensive. It's fucked."

"I don't think so."

"Think again."

We paused in front of a wild pig, tied to one of the stilts that held a thatched roof hut. The guy let his bird climb onto the rail of the stairs. Somewhere nearby were pyramids, ruins of ancient civilizations. If Frank was in Palenque, that's where he would have hung out.

"You live here?" I asked. He nodded. "How far is Chiapas?"

"You're in Chiapas. It's a big state," he said. "Let me guess. You're looking for a good view of the eclipse. Try Chamula. Outside of San Cristobal. Five or ten hour drive, walk a few miles, wait a few days. Maybe you'll see something."

I ignored his Cheshire grin. "How long have you been here?" I asked.

"Ten years, maybe, fifteen."

"Ever met a guy named Frank? Plays guitar and...."

"I know lots of guys named Frank," he laughed. "My name's Frank. Want to go see the pyramids?"

I didn't know why he made fun of me. But I followed him anyway, out of the jungle and over a barbed wire fence. I had more questions.

We walked across a field with black cows staring at us as they chewed their cud. I watched where I stepped. At the other end of the field, I squeezed barbed wire together and stood on my tiptoes to avoid getting pricked as I went over the fence.

We stood in a graveyard with wooden crosses, plastic flowers, and tiny gravestones so overgrown with green that you could hardly see them, so close together that the bodies they marked must have been quite short.

"I'm not really Frank," the guy said, suddenly getting honest. "Name's Skylar." Skylar stared at me and I looked away. "So you're famous," he said.

I thought of the movie and broke out into a whole new kind of sweat. Could it be out in Mexico already?

My eyes scanned the graveyard, avoiding Skylar's stare. I suddenly realized there were pictures of me, nailed to every tree in sight.

It was evidently part of Curso's brilliant new strategy. A circus poster with a drawing of me in front of a target, legs spread eagle, arms open like a cross. The point of view was from between Ana's legs, upwards, so it showed her bottom covered by the jagged hem of her Robin Hood costume. And between her perfect thighs, a red-haired girl, dressed like a cocktail waitress in a cowboy bar.

"What's your name anyway?"

I introduced myself with the first name that came to mind. "Eva."

We walked half way up the steep stairs of the pyramid. Skylar wiped the sweat off his brow, and I looked down at the crumbling ruins.

"This was once a noble city in a golden age," Skylar said. He stood tall and pompous like this was his birthplace and these were the homes of his ancestors. I was more interested in the mystery of the whole thing.

"What do you think happened to them?" I said.

"Depletion of the soil destroyed the Mayans, probably. Years and years of planting in one place. Or maybe it was pollution. Smoke in the air from burning the fields. Or mass suicide. Who knows? There's a guy who thinks a volcano in Indonesia made a worldwide climate change and crops froze for years after. I don't know how they could ever figure it out. Mayans were addicted to chocolate. Maybe that did them in."

"Is it worth the climb?" I asked. I was soaking wet with sweat. It felt like a hundred and ten degrees.

"There's nothing up there but stucco kings with big noses. The view's the thing. Let's go around back, sit in the shade, smoke a doobie."

"Yeah, why not."

The back of the pyramid was dark, surrounded by thick deep green jungle. The step we sat on was damp and covered with bright green moss. Skylar lit up.

"You look cool in that poster, with those knives. May I ask why? Why you do it? You could get hurt."

I hadn't really thought much about it. My mind went blank when I tried to. "I think Ana knows what she's doing."

"What if she sneezed?"

I laughed. It was a nerve-wracking idea. "I haven't done it yet. Maybe I won't."

"You're committed now. Loyalty. Truth in advertising."

I took a good strong hit from the joint. I'd sworn off drugs after the last time I saw Julia, but this was just pot.

"I owe it to her. I did something awful and she forgave me. It's the least I can do."

"Must have been good. What did you do?"

I didn't answer, but the long silence wasn't quiet. The trees were filled with parrots and monkeys, and the air was swarming with mosquitoes.

Now and then I saw an ancient stone peeking out from under the fresh green blanket that seemed to grow as we sat still.

"You're a weird chick. Kind of hostile."

"I'm hostile?"

"The eclipse is next week. We leave tonight, if you want to come."

"I should give notice. You can't run away from the circus."

"I ran away with a bunch of gypsies once. Learned how to tell fortunes. Let me see your palm."

Skylar took my right hand and spread it flat in his. The wrinkles on his face twitched and frowned as his eyes ran up and down the lines of my palm.

"Is there any other way to get to San Cristobal?" I asked. It wasn't going to be easy to leave. "Maybe Monday?"

Skylar didn't answer. He was still looking at my hand, his thoughts stretched beyond now. He took a serious breath. I was alarmed.

"What's wrong?" I said.

"You know, there are pyramids all over the place. The jungle grows so fast it buries them, faster than they can dig them up."

"What did you see in my palm?"

Skylar took a deep breath and sighed. He looked at my hand

again and then into my eyes. He ran his index finger down the middle of my palm.

"This line is your lifeline."

"What's wrong with my lifeline?"

"It's...short."

I looked at my palm. My stomach dropped.

"Not that short," he said, closing my hand and gently squeezing it. "Maybe ten, fifteen more years. Who knows..."

I leaned back on the crumbling pyramid and searched the sky. It looked like it might rain.

"Will I get married?"

Skylar looked at my hand again. "Definitely. Children? One, maybe even two."

I laughed. "Guess I'll live through the knife throwing act."

"I don't believe this stuff. You'll probably outlive me."

"Great," I said and stood up. "I've got to go."

I hated to act like I was in a hurry, it was so American. But I needed to eat before the show. Josefa always said that Indians were smart because of something in the beans. If I was going to die young, the least I could do was get smart.

Skylar stood up, too. "You want to see where they sacrificed the virgins?"

"Maybe later."

It was probably just after noon as I walked toward the town. The humidity was nearly more than I could take. The air was so thick it was like walking through water.

A donkey, with his head stuck through the barbed wire, ate grass on the other side of the fence. By the donkey, on the fence post, was my picture. The closer I got to town the more posters I saw. Anyone who visited the pyramids would surely see my likeness, advertising Curso's circus. Monkeys and donkeys would even know who I was. I heard myself laugh, not quite sure how I felt about this day.

The graveyard was much larger than I had thought. It seemed to go on forever over small rolling hills with wild green foliage that seemed to move below my feet as I walked.

In the distance was the small church we had passed on the way to the pyramids. And next to a small stone wishing well with a tarnished bell where the bucket would be, stood a gathering of people throwing handfuls of dirt into a hole in the ground. The men wore big hats and colorful sashes around their waists. The women wore black lace and cried.

I was dripping with sweat and dying of thirst. I stopped for a moment and sat on a rock to rest.

I saw a woman in the distance dressed in orange. I watched as she approached the churchyard. The woman walked quickly and for a moment I thought she must be late for the funeral. She paused at the stone wishing well. I wished it were a real well with pure fresh drinking water.

Near the open grave, beside the priest, a man in dark dirty clothing swayed back and forth, both hands reaching up to the clouds. The clouds were low and full of water, and the stone I sat on was damp. It occurred to me that it might not be okay to sit there; the stone could be marking a grave. I didn't want to sit on anybody's grave, so I got up.

As I walked toward the church, I saw the woman's pale skin and tight orange pants and her big white hat, its bright yellow scarf streaming down. She was not dressed right for a funeral. The way she moved felt unbelievably familiar to me.

The priest began to pray. Everyone closed their eyes and lowered their heads. My eyes stayed open as I walked toward the woman who did not belong at this funeral. She did not even belong in Mexico. This woman was terribly, horribly, frightfully out of place.

"Sean, oh Sean," she yelled, tripping in the dirt as she ran towards me. "Oh my baby."

A man with a dirty white tunic hummed a drunk, moaning song.

An old lady with a black lace shawl let out a long wailing cry.

The priest finished praying and everyone looked up, as my mother threw her arms around me and buried her head in my long hair.

"You won't believe what I've been through," she cried. "I was so afraid you were dead."

I hugged my momma and rested in her embrace for a brief moment.

She held me at arms' length and shook me gently. She was laughing and tears rolled down her cheeks.

"You look just like your pictures, honey. You're just as beautiful as your stills."

The people at the funeral looked on, not annoyed, but certainly interrupted.

Beside my foot were live flowers in a tin coffee can. I realized I was standing on a damp mound of dirt, someone's fresh grave. There were dead people all over the place. Dead people and a phony wishing well which, as far as I was concerned, had no business in a graveyard.

We walked back to the hotel and sat down in the crowded restaurant. I hadn't eaten in a restaurant for a long time. I considered ordering a hamburger or a Caesar salad, but it was, after all, Palenque, and not Mexico City. I ordered enchiladas.

"You're not going to believe it, honey, but all our dreams are coming true," Eudora said, as her margarita arrived. "That's why I had to come get you. Aside from the fact I was worried sick. I kept turning on the news to see if a girl was found dismembered or beheaded or god knows."

Mom shook her head in mock horror. She really did look like she'd been through the ringer, and I felt terrible that I hadn't written.

"Jack was worried, too, you know. The cops didn't help at all. We finally had to hire a detective, who found out you'd flown to Mazatlán. So I bought a ticket and went down there, with Jorge, the detective. I found your friend the veterinarian and he told me you'd run off with some *snake* handler."

"You actually hired a detective?" I said, at once embarrassed, appalled, and flattered.

"What was I supposed to do, Sean?" Mom shook her head and wrinkled her brow and licked a finger full of salt from the rim of her margarita glass. "Who is that *Curso* anyway and why did his mother feel like she had to entertain me all afternoon? You know honey, I've heard in some of these countries, they keep mistresses. And when their wives get too old, the mistresses have the men's *babies*. You'd be really sorry if you ever had kids with a Mexican man, because you can't leave. The children belong to the men."

The restaurant was crowded and I was confused. It was hard to focus on what my mother was saying. My mind wandered while Eudora ordered herself another drink and kept talking.

"Anyway, darling, they singled you out in the reviews, and that William Morris agent, remember, the one who liked me? Well, he's been calling; he has interviews up the ya-ya for Sean Hayes. I personally think you should change your name, while you still can, to Shawna. I think it's sexier. I'm telling you, a woman's life is short. This is our big chance. You can't waste your time getting killed by some jealous wife in Mexico."

My enchiladas arrived and after the waiter left, Eudora leaned across the table and whispered. "Do you know that my sources inform me that your Frank has a gun. <u>And</u> a girlfriend, honey. I'm not kidding. It's a dangerous situation. I don't know what you've gotten yourself mixed up in. Her brother, it seems, was some kind of rabble-rouser and got himself shot. And now the girl, Frank's girlfriend, is half-crazy, oh I don't know, you just need to get home. You're too beautiful for all this. It's just not safe. First thing tomorrow, I'm buying your ticket."

"There are reasons I left home, Mom. I was having a hard time."

Mom took a sip of her drink and made a face like it was too sour. "Oh god, what are you talking about Sean? In fact if Aero México is open, you know they keep such strange hours here..."

"I'm not leaving yet. I have a job. Are you coming to the show tonight?"

".....I've already checked the times. Tuesday morning at six thirty-three a.m."

"Count me out."

"Six in the morning is not the time I usually like to travel, but I'll buy you breakfast in Mexico City and..."

"Mother, did you hear me? I'm not ready to leave."

"...let's see, we arrive in Mexico City at eight, and mind you we have to fly on a horrible little plane....."

"Stop it!"

"But we'll be home by dinner and Jack..."

I put a finger in each ear, closed my eyes, and screamed at the top of my lungs.

I was as shocked as she was. But it worked. The entire restaurant was silenced, including my mother.

I finished my soup, wiped my mouth with the cloth napkin and very politely said, "I have to go now. I have a show to do."

My mother smiled, as if we had just concluded a lovely meal. "What role, exactly, do you play in this circus?" she asked.

The animals trotted around the ring. The circus music sounded lively as ever. Enrique seemed to feel better. I didn't.

It was time for Ana's knife debut and my first performance as a lovely human target. We'd never had a rehearsal, for as Ana explained, knives were never practiced on a live target. Live targets were used only in performance.

I entered the ring. The fringe that ran along the bottom of my cowgirl skirt costume tickled my inner thighs. The drums rumbled and rolled.

I climbed onto the fake grass platform and leaned against the red bulls-eye. I slipped my feet into the small straps and spread my arms, like I'd seen myself do in the poster.

The Pink Lady entered and took stage. The leather straps that ran down her thighs were filled with shining blades. She bowed dramatically. The music seemed to grow louder and faster. Cymbals clanged and drums pounded, at once terrifying and exciting, an incessant, driving dream.

Ana took a firm stance several yards in front of me; feet together, back straight, almost military. I felt as if I'd been challenged to a duel. But I had no weapon.

Ana pulled a knife from her belt and aimed it, like an arrow in a taut bow, pointed at my neck.

The blade cut through the air with a whizzing sound. My toes curled in their slippers, clinging to their tiny metal platforms. The knife landed just above my shoulder.

Ana's face scrunched up, her lips got thinner. She let go of another weapon and then another. One landed to the left of my arm and the next one beside my hand. My blood pumped fast.

Ana's intense glare was real. The warm soft eyes I had known were gone.

Knife after knife landed with a whoosh. I counted, one, two, three, up the side of my body. Four, five, six, down to my foot. Soaking wet and frozen stiff, I prayed it would soon be over. Seven, eight, up the inside of my leg, nine, near the top of my inner thigh. How many more could there be?

My mother sat stiff in the audience, paying strict attention. She must have felt my eyes on her because she started waving with both hands and throwing me kisses.

A blade cut into the target right below my crotch. Ana's teeth glistened.

I promised myself I would never trust anyone again. As I felt the next knife land close to my waist, I closed my eyes and laughed at the idea that anyone could hurt or scare me.

Then I began to imagine a new place for myself. I knew how to get out of the here and now. That is one thing I knew how to do. We learn things when we are small, all sorts of things we never forget. Once in a while, they come in handy.

I saw myself from way above, where I floated on the surface of the deep warm sea, looking down at tropical fish, friendly crustaceans, and tiny silver submarines that, one by one, framed a strange girl's flesh.

The crowd stood and cheered as the final knife flew toward my head like a bird flapping in wondrous slow motion. Ana took bow after bow and the knife still vibrated against my ear.

I slipped my arms out of the straps and calmly undid my legs. My relief was quickly followed by a surge of rage.

My eyes shot over to Ana. Her smile was large and bold and directly at me. Her eyes shone like the eyes of a wolf in the woods.

I ran out behind the tent. I leaned against the cab of the semi truck. My body shook all over.

Ana came up beside me and touched my arm. Her hands burned my skin. I wouldn't look at her.

"You didn't take your bow," she said.

I stared at the ground and clenched my jaw. Behind me, tied to the truck, Enrique rattled his chain.

Ana moved my chin, gently, so I had to face her.

"You are angry," she said. "You think I put you in danger."

"You could have killed me, that's all."

"Circus work is always dangerous. Tigers, elephants, trapeze. I posed for knives myself."

I tried to yank my arm away, but Ana wouldn't let go. She looked like a cartoon witch. Her porcelain stage make-up had cracked in deep wrinkles that I had never before noticed.

"You're crazy..," I said, "... like the rest of the world."

I heard the audience letting out. Enrique rumbled a deep moan.

He was still in costume and he brushed against the truck repeatedly, trying to rub the gold sequined hat off the top of his head.

I saw Curso point my mother in my direction.

"I am sorry, I didn't mean to hurt you," Ana said. "I desperately needed this new act."

I wondered if it was sweat or tears that made Ana's eye make-up run down her cheeks. She didn't look like a witch anymore, but she sure wasn't wearing a halo. I had imagined that Ana was the wise and loving woman I had always longed for, someone who would protect me from anything. Maybe such creature didn't exist, at least not since Grandma died. My jaw ached and there was a horrible taste in my mouth.

"Good God, that was wonderful, so dramatic," yelled my mother, rushing towards me with two pink balloons tied to her Louis Vuitton bag.

She grabbed Ana's hand. "You are such a fabulous performer. Those knives look absolutely real. I got chills, swear to God. I've never seen anything like it. Sean, I have a terrific idea for some publicity we could do...."

Suddenly Enrique picked up his foot and yanked. The chain broke like torn tissue. He walked, carefully at first, a few steps from the truck, and then fast, right past us. The streaks under his eyes that usually looked like tear tracks, now resembled war paint.

The elephant broke out into a thundering run.

There was chaos around the tents as the word spread. Curso ran back and forth shouting, "¡EL ELEFANTE SE ESCAPO!"

Guns appeared out of nowhere. It seemed as if there were hundreds of men with rifles, running in every direction.

I went back to my trailer to change clothes and gather my things. Not that I had much. A few T-shirts, a pair of jeans, the dress Josefa made me, the earrings Señora de León gave me, and the hat that Frank loved. I took off the soaking wet cowgirl costume and put my dress and boots back on.

I stuck Ana's purple leotard in the bag. I told myself I'd earned it, but I wondered if I was stealing. I left the cowgirl costume on the floor.

I wanted to say good-bye to my mother. But she would have caused a scene; she wouldn't have let me go easy. I could see her, standing back by the tents, holding her pretty pink balloons and calling my name. She looked absolutely lost, like a two-year-old alone in a crowded mall.

A huge crowd had gathered on the road by the little market. Cars full of federales arrived. A small uniformed man shouted orders through a megaphone. Curso kept interrupting him.

The federale slammed the megaphone down. He walked straight up to Curso.

"Silencio y sientate!" he shouted, spitting in Curso's face as he told him to shut up and sit down.

Curso stepped up into the cab of his truck and folded his hands humbly onto his lap.

Skylar came out of the store with his bird on his shoulder and a bag full of supplies in his arms. He had seen the show and was expecting me. "You coming?" he said.

I adjusted my blue hat and waved at Curso, who sat, chastised, in the cab of his truck with the door wide open. He kind of shrugged and waved back. His face looked worn and guilty. He looked to me like an overgrown boy, who knew that in his life he had stolen more attention than he deserved.

The plastic was torn off the seats of Skylar's Volkswagen, leaving naked foam rubber. The door was ripped off the glove box, the radio was missing.

Skylar started the car. His bird was on the headrest and an iguana was on his lap.

"So much for believing you can't tame wild animals," I said.

"I haven't tamed nothing. These guys are still wild." The iguana crawled halfway up Skylar's chest and rested, blinking.

Before we could pull out, a big Pepsi truck turned in front of the market from the main road, onto the cobblestone where we were parked. The truck leaned as it turned, and two cases of soda crashed onto the ground in front of us.

The driver parked his truck in the middle of the street, blocking our car, as he retrieved the plastic cases. Another car pulled up behind us and the Pepsi driver started chatting with the guy in the car.

Traffic backed up. The old lady from the store came out to watch and told the Pepsi man about the wild, dangerous elephant. They stood in the street speaking in hushed and worried tones as they leisurely kicked broken Pepsi bottles off the road.

Drivers sat patiently behind their steering wheels and stared straight ahead, as if they were at an outdoor movie. I kept looking behind us to see if anyone was coming after me. The slow pace of Mexico that had once seemed so relaxed now felt idiotic.

The Pepsi driver finally moved his truck, and the four or five car pile-up started to disperse. As we sputtered onto the highway, I saw townsfolk gathered in front of the store, sending each other off in different directions. I wondered why they were all so upset. It seemed to me that the jungle was a fine place for an elephant to live.

13

Thousand-Year-Old Song

SOON IT WAS ON EVERY radio station. A mad elephant had broken loose from the circus and virtually destroyed a small village before disappearing into the jungle. They said he'd killed two grown men, one of whom had been seated inside his own living room, peacefully watching television.

We'd driven on one road for three bumpy hours before finding it was closed, due to torrential downpours, and we had to backtrack. When we finally entered the town of San Cristobal, it just after noon and we'd been on the road for seventeen hours total, including time spent napping in the car.

Skylar was acting like a jerk. He had decided to stay on the road for eight more hours and watch the eclipse on a beach with some friends. He wanted company and I wanted to be dropped off.

"What's so special about Frank?" he asked.

"What's it to you?" I said. There was an angry edge to my voice that I hadn't really intended.

"You're just going from one sorry situation to another. You're lucky that elephant didn't kill you."

A few days before, I would have told him that he was way off base, that Enrique might hurt other people, but he would never have hurt me. Today, I said nothing.

Skylar told me a woman named Jo at a place call Na-kaloom would know where any foreigners were. He dropped me off, said, "See ya around," and motioned toward the general direction I should go. Then he sped away. I stood alone on a five-spoked corner and took a guess at which street he meant.

The sidewalk was so narrow I had to step into a doorway to let a woman with two small children pass. The door behind me opened and a white guy wearing huarache sandals slid past me. I stopped him to ask where I might find Na-Kaloom. "Right here," he said in English with a German accent. He disappeared down the sidewalk.

The thick double mahogany door was slightly ajar, so I slipped through it, gently pushing a stray dog with my foot as I shut him out. I found myself in a courtyard, stark and bare, a stone square with arches and many doors. The door to my left was open and I walked into a room lined with books. A large glass cabinet was filled with very old photographs of dark men dressed in un-bleached cloth.

A woman appeared in the doorway. She had gray-white hair and wore a faded huipil.

"Can I help you?" she asked. She sounded like she was from the States, but looked like she'd lived here forever.

"I'm searching for a guy named Frank."

"Does this look like a lost and found?" Her gray curls made me think of a country and western singer. A singer, like Frank.

My eyes scanned the bookshelves that reached all the way to the ceiling and back down to the floor. I didn't want to leave; I didn't know where I'd go.

"So many books....." I said.

"Are you all right?"

"Can I maybe stay for a little while?"

She thought about it a moment, and looked at me intently.

"Who are you?"

It was a big question. I took time with it before I didn't answer.

"You stay for supper," she said.

It was more an order than an invitation. I nodded. I was glad that I hadn't just spouted off something from the top of my head.

I took a book off the shelf, brown and old. The pages inside smelled smoky, sweet and soothing. Inside were photos of Mayan ruins, and pages filled with drawings of the Mayans' written language. I was fascinated by the glyphs, arranged in columns that looked like totem poles. Fantasy animals with wide-open mouths, profiles of bearded wolf-men with curly noses, a smiling elephant with a hat but no trunk. I sat down and tried to make sense of it all.

The communal dining table was elegant in a rustic sort of way. The chairs were wood and none of them matched. Several people spoke politely in different languages. The food was passed family style and out of order, coffee first, then salad and vegetables.

Jo sat at the head of the table and poured coffee. On either side of her, across from each other, sat a young couple, blond with rosy cheeks like they had lived in clean air. An older man and his male companion, a young studious type, spoke French to the couple, but Jo spoke to them in German.

I sat at the other end of the table, beside a local man in an undyed tunic. Two women were at his left. One held a young child, the other nursed an infant. The older woman chewed food and transferred it to her child's mouth in what might have seemed a kiss. The man had black shiny hair that hung down his chest and reminded me of Frank's. They spoke to each other in an Indian language.

Jo finally looked toward me as I paused at the salad bowl that had been passed. "You can eat the lettuce here. I grow it in my garden. So what did you find in my library? Did you read anything that interested you?"

"I didn't read, really. I looked at the hieroglyphs."

Jo nodded. "Ah, ancient words, lost stories."

"Don't they know what the glyphs mean?"

"A few have been deciphered. Dates, some names. We may never know the whole story of the Mayans."

The young Indian woman dipped a spoon into the sugar bowl and poured a heaping spoonful of sugar into her man's fourth or fifth cup of coffee. Her breast fell out of her infant's mouth and the baby struggled in its sleep to find the nipple again. The woman ignored the baby's wiggling head as she added one spoon after another, until she'd added six or seven spoons of sugar to the single cup of coffee she then tasted.

The lettuce on my tongue was like cool fresh butter. I savored the lightly cooked carrots and corn and rice. I hadn't had an American meal in so long. Dessert was homemade ice cream with the richest vanilla I'd ever tasted.

"Our friends here are the Kayums. They are Lacandon Indians, descendants of a wandering Maya who were never conquered," Jo said.

"Is that his wife?" The blond lady asked in a heavy accent.

"They are both his wives."

The younger woman looked at me shyly as she spooned sugar into her own coffee.

The man's dark eyes stole mine in a curious search that was at once so innocent and so sexy that it sent a long and pleasing chill through my body.

Jo walked me through the courtyard and into her office. Her desk was covered with neat stacks of photos and papers. She handed me a pen and a makeshift Xeroxed book with the latest translations from Mayan glyphs.

"Copy these, it is calming. It will heal you. We study here, that is what we do. Come, I will show you to your room. You may stay for a night or two."

The room was large and cool. Crude musical instruments decorated the walls. The bed was high and piled with a fluffy down comforter. The fireplace was stacked with wood and paper, all ready to be lit.

In the corner was a trunk, dark green metal, wrapped with two leather belts.

"Evangelina left her things here. Please don't bother them. She'll be back, I never know when. Strange girl, Evangelina, lost little orphan, rarely speaks." Jo lit a match and started the fire. "Breakfast is at eight, dinner also. You may bring books to your room, but no men." She closed the door.

I sank into the big chair with my book, ready to read by firelight. The hieroglyphics fascinated me. Squares with rounded edges, profiles of men with large noses and low lidded eyes. Lazy cynical parrots and stairs leading to the sky. Hands curled into fists and smiling frogs.

Motherfather, it said beside one glyph, the earth's creator. One word. Motherfather.

I copied the glyph, over and over. Just drawing it took me to a mysterious state of mind and body, suspended in a slower world, far away in time. For a moment I felt relaxed and peaceful.

I lay on the bed and drifted into a fantasy of running away with the Kayum man. We would live in a tall forest and make love outdoors. I wouldn't care that he had other women, for I would have naked babies sleeping all around. Cuddled up behind me, sweet round bottoms snuggled against my back, tiny moist lips sucking on my breasts, soft silky legs curled into my tummy. I wouldn't have to travel, wouldn't have to look for anyone. I would be warm and comfortable and satisfied.

The fire burned low. I put another log on and waited to see if the embers would light it.

My eyes fixed on the trunk sitting in the corner, the one I wasn't so supposed to touch. I bolted the door and dragged it out into the room. I undid the belts and felt only a tinge of guilt as I opened it.

Inside, a couple of T-shirts, a huipil, a pair of old jeans, a notebook, and stacks and stacks of drawings. Drawings of trees, lone trees, fallen trees, loggers, forests. One was a drawing of a dozen fallen trees and each one had a face, faint and camouflaged in the bark.

Stuffed in the corner of the trunk was a piece of paper crushed into a ball. I picked it up, uncrumpled it. It was a drawing that wasn't a tree, a picture of a mother and child, naked, blissful. The mother had a scar across her breast. But her face was a man's. It was Frank. It was definitely Frank.

I ran into the courtyard to see if anyone was around. A light came out of a room near the library. I knocked on the door and heard laughter from inside. Jo opened the door. I held the drawing of Frank in my hand.

"This is the guy I'm looking for. I found it under the bed."

Jo looked at the drawing and smiled. "So?"

"I need to find him. He's waiting for me."

Jo turned and said something in French to the blond couple who were laughing on the couch behind her. The room smelled of brandy and tobacco and a sweet burning wood.

"What's funny?" I asked. It felt like they were laughing at me.

"Nothing. They're just in love. So you really want to see Frank?"

"Where is he?"

"The Kayums go home tomorrow. They are taking two anthropologists with them. Frank stays at a place on the way. I'm sure they won't mind if you go along."

At first the morning had been brilliant. On the narrow sidewalk, I walked behind the Indian women, who trailed their husband, carrying baskets full of supplies on their heads and babies on their backs. I'd thought the Kayums would lead us to a bus or a car, but they just kept walking and I followed, through the town, uphill, and when the town ended, uphill still, on a long dirt road.

The sky was wide -- nothing stood in its way. Behind us, the town was a blanket of purple, blossoms of the Jacarandas. Yellow flowers filled the countryside. Once in a while we'd pass a cluster of houses, their yards filled with children and pigs and chickens. Kayum's legs were brown and strong. I could hear my footsteps and they made me smile. It was nice to think that someone knew where we were going.

But as morning turned to noon and noon got close to dinnertime, my feet began to hurt. The Kayum ladies giggled together, and the blond couple chattered in German, but no one spoke to me. The sun still burned hot, and the tiny cornfields beside the tin houses looked sad and scorched.

A brown and gray splotchy dog with a bloody chewed-up tail and a red spot on his nose followed me out of a village. He looked diseased and I didn't want to touch him, but he knew I felt sorry for him because I didn't kick him or yell "Get," so he kept coming closer. If I could just get it out of my head that I felt so sorry for him, he might quit following me. But I couldn't.

The walk had become painful and frightening, and I could barely see the trail. I was hot and hungry and had begun to wonder where I'd sleep that night. The dog nipped at my ankle and whined. The road stank of dung.

"God damn you stupid fucking dog," I yelled, stomping towards him. He ran away, terrified, with his tail between his legs and a guilty look on his face.

Kayum stopped at a T in the road. He pointed off to the right, and made a sign with his hands that was a measure of distance. I had no idea what it meant, but I waved good-bye and walked on by myself. The sky had turned pink. The only sounds were insects. I was lonely and scared and now I missed the dog.

I finally came to a long stretch of chicken wire and an old wooden gate. I don't know how I knew this was it. As I opened the gate, I thought that it was a moment I would always remember. I imagined that the memory would be like the picture at Grandma's of Jesus opening the gate to your heart.

Down a green slope in a small valley was a crude stucco house with a tin roof, and another small building, odd-shaped with no ceiling. An emerald green pond lay between them and behind the whole area was a forest of trees. By the pond was a thatched roof hut and under it, on a wooden bench, sat a man in a brown suede jacket. He seemed to be listening, intently, to music I couldn't hear.

My heard pounded. It was certainly Frank. He was alone.

It took all of my strength not to burst into tears and run into his arms. My nose tickled and burned. It was the end of a long journey.

When he finally felt that he was being watched, Frank was startled. He jumped up and grabbed a gun that had been leaning on the post beside him. He looked around lost, wondering which way to point his rifle.

Squinting his eyes against the setting sun, it dawned on him that it was only me.

"Jesus," he said, setting the gun down. "You scared the shit out of me."

His voice was a low breeze at dusk, warm as the Santa Anas. He chuckled, deeply nervous, because he hadn't seen me in so long. But he didn't run towards me. He just shook his head back and forth, smiling like Stevie Wonder, lost in his own soulful song.

His lips were slightly parted and his jacket looked slept in. I was dying to run my hands over his unshaven face.

"Is that really you, Sean?" Frank asked.

I shrugged and a twitch moved through me in an upward jerking motion. Suddenly I felt awkward in my body, no longer a gymnast's body like it had been in Ana's costume. It was just a skinny piece of flesh, breastless and out of place.

His eyes held mine and wouldn't let go. They looked so deep, I thought I might fall in.

"It is you," Frank said.

"As far as I know."

Frank didn't laugh. He knew how far I'd walked and he was worried about me. "You okay?"

My throat knotted up. "Sure."

"You don't look like you did in the photo."

"You saw the posters?"

"I saw you in a magazine. You're a movie star."

"I am? In Mexico? What magazine?" I wondered what kind of pictures they'd printed, but I didn't dare ask. I was confused and dizzy with sweat.

"Hey, you sure you're okay?" Frank asked. He looked so concerned, I felt like I might collapse in his arms. "You want to lie down? Come on over here." The smell of Frank's coat was musty and warm, like sea salt and body heat and Mexican dust.

He helped me climb into a hammock that was strung between two trees by the pond. The high grass gently tickled my naked legs. Two little brown birds wet their beaks in a puddle just below the hammock. They too, I imagined, had come from farther north, from a land even colder than anywhere I had ever been.

I was awakened by cool rain on my face. I ran back to the shed, not bothering to dry off because it was still warm outside, and it felt good to be a little wet. I was surprised to find the table set and a fire burning on the stone stove.

Frank sat there, where he'd been when I fell asleep, hunched over his guitar, like a tired old soul.

"You hungry?" he asked.

I nodded. He filled a blue metal cup from the pot on the stove and handed it to me, full of steaming rice and kernels of corn.

I looked around for a spoon or fork. There was an old wooden shelf with a few dishes and utensils on the other side, but Frank was silent and I was afraid to bother him. After all, he'd cooked this whole meal and waited for me to wake up.

He filled his cup and picked up a spoon for himself. He sat down at the table and ate his dinner.

I licked a few pieces of rice from the edge of my cup.

"If the universe doubled, you think anyone would notice?" Frank asked.

"Sure. Everything would be heavier, right?"

"No, I mean in time, doubled in time."

"I guess we'd live longer."

"For better or worse."

I looked beyond the shed to see if anyone else was around.

Frank reached out, and with the backs of his fingers stroked my cheek. "You have the softest, palest, most beautiful skin I've ever seen," he said.

He finished eating without saying another word. Then he stood up, slammed his cup down on the table, and walked off toward the house.

I used his spoon and ate my dinner.

There were two rooms in the stucco house. One had a bed and a lantern. The other was tiny, with space only for a hammock like the one outside. The rooms were separated by a doorway with no door.

I looked for signs of Evangelina, Eva, the girl who had drawn Frank. But I saw nothing that indicated she was around.

Frank sat on the bed with his knees bent and his arms cradling his guitar, which now had just three strings. He strummed a song as his head swayed slowly left to right. His eyes tilted down, slightly sleepy and soft brown in the lamplight.

I lay on the bed beside him and stared at the ceiling while Frank stroked his guitar. The simple melody was more beautiful than a woman could ever be.

I wanted to take the guitar from his arms.

"New song?" I said.

"Written a thousand years ago."

Frank leaned his guitar against the wall, and lay back down beside me, carefully making sure our bodies didn't touch. The lantern sent shadows playing upon the ceiling.

"I'm going to this place where everyone sings harmony in the streets. In the mountains of Java or Sumatra, I can't remember exactly where. But I'm going there." Frank's voice sounded like an angel that longed for heaven.

He sat up again, suddenly, and pulled a small tape recorder out of the pocket of his suede jacket.

"Want to hear a recording I made?" He sat on the edge of the bed, his back towards me. "Listen to this," he said.

First there was nothing, then, a scratching sound, dull and deep, and then, a woman's voice. It was distant and the lyrics were incomprehensible.

We listened together, exchanging magical glances like children who shared a secret in the dark. The connection that our eyes made completed a circuit.

Frank shut the tape off.

"I heard it in an ancient vase," he said.

Frank looked for my reaction. I moved slightly beside him on the bed, so that our thighs lightly touched. Frank stared at the tape recorder; he wouldn't look at me.

I placed my hand lightly on top of his, but he instantly flicked it off, as if an insect stung him.

"You should have come sooner," he said. His voice was so full of rage, it made me flinch. His anger told me that I mattered. It gave me a rush I could feel all through my body.

"I couldn't find you. You didn't say exactly where you were going."

"You could've found me, if you cared." He spoke slowly and his breath was loud and heavy.

"Oh God, Frank, I do care, I really care."

Frank stared hard into my eyes, as if trying to read my soul. The lamplight flickered in his dark eyes. I sat very, very still. I wanted him to grab me, dig in, like in my fantasies, and kiss me hard.

But he just grabbed his guitar.

He played for a moment, then changed his mind, put it down and picked up the lantern.

"Did you hear about the guy who killed himself in a hotel room, and left a note, saying he just couldn't stand the flowered curtains?"

"Is that supposed to be funny?" I said, trying in vain to swing with his moods.

Frank walked into the next room. "You want the bed or the hammock?"

"Whatever," I shrugged, following him.

He handed me a blanket from the closet and showed me how to lie diagonally in the hammock. "It's more comfortable," he said. "You don't sink down as much."

I studied the knotted rope and the nail that secured the hammock and wondered if it would hold the weight of two, if Frank were to climb in with me. But he didn't. He snuffed the lantern out and went into the other room.

The small window next to me had no glass. It was just a square hole, letting cool air in. I held the blanket close.

Outside the window, I thought I saw a figure, peeking from behind a tree. I told myself it was only in my head, that I was really safe.

I awoke to a loud thud right outside. Through the tiny window I saw a girl turn from the sink. She held an ax in one hand and a chicken upside down in the other, still flapping its wings, blood pouring from its neck. She dropped the headless chicken in a bucket and disappeared beyond the trees.

I slipped out of the hammock, trying to sort out where I was, what was real and what was still a dream. I had slept in my dress. I looked around for a mirror, but the room was bare. I ran my fingers through my hair and went outside.

On the barbed wire fence, below my bedroom window, hung a pair of jeans, a couple of old t-shirts and a dress. I touched the faded blue cloth of the dress. A sinking feeling wanted me.

Frank sat on the bench, guitar in his lap, a yellow pad on the wooden table in front of him. He strummed a few chords, wrote something down, and barely noticed as I sat across from him.

I ate a piece of bread, silently, while he drank hot coffee and rubbed his unshaved face.

"Listen," he said.

I listened and knew exactly what he was talking about - the music of insects. The leaves rustled gently and the monarch butterflies fluttered, happy in the breeze after their thousand-mile flight south.

"That's where the song is," Frank whispered. He stared at me. A soft wind swirled lightly over my skin and made me shiver.

"Who is the girl?"

"A friend. Eva."

An iguana crawled into the shade under the table.

"She draws pictures of you?"

Frank didn't answer.

"She's just a friend now?"

The dead chicken made a horrible noise. I leaned to the side a little and saw it, back by the pump, still flopping about. Blood and feathers were scattered around the bucket, under the sink.

I asked again. "She's just a friend?"

Frank set his guitar down very deliberately. "I can't write," he said. "You're making this so fucking hard."

"I'm sorry."

"What's wrong with you?"

"I'm sorry."

I wondered why I apologized. All I'd done was ask a question.

"Maybe something's wrong with you," I said under my breath.

Frank stood up suddenly, knocking the bench over.

"Damn you!" He reared his foot back and kicked an ancient vase, shattering it. I shielded my face as broken pieces of pottery flew all over the place.

"Frank?" I said softly. "You're scaring me."

Frank got right up in my face and glared at me like I was a despicable murderer.

"We should all be scared, Sean."

I froze, my slight smile begging for a response. A huge red ant crawled up my leg. I squished it between my fingers and flicked it off.

Frank paced like an agitated lion.

It's a good idea to get out of the way sometimes. I learned some things at home.

Out back, by the pump, the dead chicken's head sat on the sink, one eye still wide open. The body had stopped moving. I pulled it out of the bucket and poured the blood onto the ground. I stuck the body into a big pot. I pumped water into a pan and carried it around to the fire.

Frank had disappeared. Pottery lay in pieces all over the ground.

I poured boiling water over the chicken and soaked it so I could pluck its feathers. I cleaned up the broken vase. It smelled like earth and when I held it to my ear, there was definitely a sound, a low hum, like way underground, far beneath the ocean.

I cut up the onions and tomatoes that had been washed by the girl, Eva, I supposed, and sat waiting on the sink. The chicken's eye blinked. I closed my own eyes, picked up his head by its comb and tossed it into the bushes.

I pulled feather after feather out of the bird's flesh. I boiled the chicken and poured rice into the pot. I slipped carrots one by one into the water. It seemed like it might make soup. I had never cooked on an outdoor stove. I had never really cooked at all. But I was glad that I had learned from Grandma how to pluck a chicken raw.

My soup tasted rich and warm, like home in a cup. I almost felt okay alone. Then I thought I heard Frank talking.

I took my cup and followed the sound toward the shack on the other side of the pond. As I got closer, I realized he was singing.

Frank called it his Nighthouse, but it wasn't a house at all. It looked like a shack that had been abandoned before it was ever finished. There was no roof and the walls were tall, but I had to hunch over to get through the door.

The room inside was maybe six feet square. Frank sat in the corner, bent over his guitar, plucking the smoky slow ending to his song.

After he finished, I handed him the cup of soup. He smiled, so I eased down beside him. The wall in front of us was made of thick, rough-looking wood planks. No windows, no ceiling in the Nighthouse, just four walls.

"This place is like a fort," Frank said. "And there's no roof, so we can watch the eclipse from here."

He scooted down and lay back onto the naked ground. He hadn't put in a floor either, and I didn't dare insult him by asking if he planned to. Maybe he thought bare ground was enough. You never know in Mexico, you never knew with Frank.

"How do you watch an eclipse?" I asked. "Don't we need a filter or something? So we don't go blind?"

"I have goggles. But when the moon covers the sun completely, you can watch with your naked eye. And you can always listen, of course. There's a song with every miracle. Therein lies the ultimate truth."

Frank paused for a few moments and we looked up at the night sky.

"I used to think the answers were in ancient recordings." Frank's voice was low and wise, like a bearded old man. "But that was far too scientific. By the time the potter's wheel got to Mexico, truth was terrified. Truth saw the future and hid in silence. Now, truth is beyond words. Like making love or dying."

I knew exactly what he meant, staring out at the heavens, so deep and dark, with more stars than I had ever seen.

"You don't see many stars in L.A.," I sighed.

"There were a lot where I grew up," Frank said. "When my folks fought, I'd go outside, and wander around. The sky had lights."

"Wish I'd gone outside. I hid under the bed. Scared to move. Somebody might get hurt." I laughed.

Frank looked very serious, as if he felt pity for me. "What's so funny about that?" he said.

I looked inside myself, to see why I had laughed, and why Frank felt so sorry for me. I felt like I'd fallen down an elevator shaft.

Frank hummed a soft melody, at once soothing and terrifying. He cupped his hand under my chin and lifted my face, so I could see the sky and know that its vast darkness is so much larger than my fear.

"Aren't we ever going to make love again?" I blurted out.

Frank shook his head.

"Why not? Because of Eva?" I had to ask fast before my boldness ran out.

He shook his head again.

"Then why not?"

Frank took my question seriously and bit the inside of his cheek as he thought about it for a long time.

"You get connected," he said. "And after that, you get to know each other. Maybe you don't like each other. But you're stuck."

"We know each other," I said, a slight question mark tainting my argument.

Frank looked like he'd thought of something that just irritated him.

"Not really," he shrugged, as if suddenly bored. "Just wait." He let out a breathy chuckle and looked my way out of the corner of his eye, with the sexiest glint I had ever seen.

His words told me one thing but his eyes sang another.

I had to make it happen. I just had to.

The moon had crevices that night, places I could fall into if I thought too much or wished too hard.

I lay awake in my hammock until the sun rose and the birds started to sing. I heard Frank toss around in the next room and I waited. I heard him pull himself up and lean against his pillow, I heard him bend down and get the yellow pad from the floor beside him.

I climbed out of my hammock and walked into his room. I wore only panties.

I sat on his bed. Scared, timid, I placed my hand upon his thigh. He dropped his yellow pad and looked at me like I was crazy.

"What are you doing?" he said.

"I don't know. Trying to be your friend."

We both sat frozen for a long time. I saw a thousand painful thoughts run through his face.

"Oh man," he said. He touched the inside of my thigh with just his fingertips. "That is so beautiful, look at that."

He let out a sigh of surrender and ran his hand between my breasts and down to my stomach.

"Wow, look at you!" he whispered. He kissed me and then slowly let go and kissed me more. And then, we made love.

It wasn't dreamy or otherworldly like the first time. But it wasn't fast and dirty, like with Curso.

It was slippery soft skin and deep damp smells. It was stark naked and unbearably bright, like sunlight in blue eyes.

Afterwards, we lay next to each other. Frank stroked my hair.

I wanted to ask him if he thought loneliness was just a need, like food and water. Or if it was a dream of something more.

I wanted to ask if his love hid in silence.

But I didn't.

I just lay naked, next to him, and let him stroke my hair, until I could hardly stand another gentle moment. I had wanted this so long, having it was almost more than I could bear.

The place inside where tenderness lives is the place that hides all pain. Tenderness lies hidden near the pain.

Alone, I woke up in Frank's bed, shaking in the dark. The wind was strong in the trees.

I wondered where he was and when he would return. I wondered if his sperm still lived inside of me and hoped one might find what it was looking for.

The night was full of noises, none of them song. Animal screeching and bellowing sounds. Once I even thought I heard wild elephants, loose in the woods, ripping trees by their roots from the ground.

I thought of counting elephants, to go to sleep. I thought of pink elephants and elephant memories and tiny little elephant minds and ivory towers and necklaces. But you can count all the elephants left in the world, and you'll run out before you fall asleep.

So I lay awake, thoughts thrashing about in my head like bumper cars going nowhere.

Rain came through the window and danced on the tin roof. I listened to the rain, but it never soothed.

The frogs and crickets clicked and croaked and the mean mosquitoes kept at me.

Dawn made me think of Enrique, wandering lost in the forest. We are all small in the wee hours of morning, when we awaken in fear and longing, and there is no shoulder to cry on, there are no arms to hold us.

14

A Lullaby For Eva

FRANK WAS NOWHERE TO BE found. It was late morning and the campesinos were burning the fields just south of us. As Skylar had explained, it was the unfortunate way they prepared the fields to plant again, depleting the soil in the process. Clouds of smoke filled the air.

I had to get out of there, get to higher ground, and find some air. I walked up the road toward a store I had seen.

It was quiet in the mountains. I tried to talk myself into a good mood. Frank would probably be back by the time I returned. I could buy sweet bread to make him feel good on his birthday. Maybe we would take a walk in the woods and talk about how special it was going to be, watching the eclipse together.

The store was a shack really, a few shelves, some morning bread, Chiclets, sodas and eggs so fresh they were still covered with chicken poop and pieces of feather. I bought three eggs and some bread. A cheery lady, with big old bosoms like my Grandma, took my coins and put them in a hardware box. She smiled and chattered away and I didn't understand a word. Behind her was a television, for all the customers and people in the village to watch. And on the screen, with a WMEX microphone in his face, was Curso.

He stood on the steps in front of his trailer while a man dressed in black-rimmed glasses interviewed him. Curso stared straight at the camera, his jet-black hair gleaming in the light, his proud grin big as a fingernail moon. Sweat glistened on his chest hairs, and he was still puffed up from performing. I strained to understand what he was saying. He was defending Enrique, explaining that he did not kill people on purpose, that he just didn't know how big he was and he was frightened like the rest of us.

It was just what I'd been thinking in the middle of the night. Everyone has their moods, Curso said. Life is just more dangerous for an elephant.

The storekeeper said something about the famous elephant who fought for his freedom. Then she gave me a candy, a brown sugar skull with shiny red eyes.

The gate creaked as I opened it. Butterflies flew out of the bushes, and darkened the sky.

Eva stood near the pond, her shining face round as the moon itself. She held a hoe over her head and slowly, methodically, swung it to the ground. Over and over it landed with a horrible crunching sound.

The snake she was hitting had long been dead, but all around were tiny live snakes. They hung from low branches of the bushes, they wiggled in the mud at the edge of the pond, they crawled around in the dirt between us.

"Where did all these baby snakes come from?" I asked.

She stared at me, smiling, ghostlike in her silence. Her deep rose lips were moist and ever so slightly opened. A stray strand of black hair fell over one eye and she swept it back with a toss of her head. Her strange beauty was unnerving. I felt awkward, staring at her, my feet surrounded by tiny wiggling reptiles.

"That snake must have been pregnant," I said.

Eva pounded the ground again with her hoe, but after a moment, she stopped. Her smile melted into a haunted look, deep circles around her eyes. She clearly didn't want to talk to me.

"No, I guess she couldn't have been pregnant. They lay eggs," I thought aloud. "Reptiles, right?"

Eva scooped up the large battered snake with the hoe and held it dangling in front of me.

I looked out at the house and down toward the tables to see if there was any sign of Frank.

"Where do you sleep?" I asked.

She pointed toward the trees.

"He used to have your name tattooed," I said, simply. "Eva, right?"

Eva tossed the dead snake into the pond and started to rake the little ones together with the hoe.

"Of course," I laughed. "You don't speak English."

I wondered how she could be such good friends with Frank, and then realized I didn't really know what his Spanish was like. "No habla Inglés. ¿verdad?" I asked.

She smiled, half-heartedly tolerant. When she spoke, it was slowly, as if teaching English to a second grader. Her accent sounded just like Ana's.

"When threatened, the mother snake swallows her young. I freed the babies."

She turned her head up to the sky and said, in a tiny singsong voice: "I swim to Frank like a baby swims back to the womb. In the dark hours of morning."

She walked very slowly, heel to toe, like a small child pretending to walk a tightrope. When she reached the pond's edge she kept going, into the muddy green water. Her blue dress rose to the surface, floating up around her body, as she sank into the pond. Her arms rested on top of the water and her head tilted back, as if she might almost relax.

But her dark eyes stayed wide open, like sunflowers with no petals.

It was late in the day, and still no sign of Frank. I ate the candy skull the shop lady with big bosoms had given me. The sugar gave me a lift.

A box of matches sat on the brick stove and some firewood lay on the ground. I stuck a few pieces in the stove. On the ground was some crumpled paper that Frank had ripped from the pad while he was writing. I tried and couldn't read it, so I put it in the stove and lit a match to it. Flames rose around the wadded sheets of yellow lined paper. The wood caught fire.

From a coffee tin, I scooped a dollop of lard and slapped it into the frying pan. The fire crackled, the grease sizzled, and I told myself it was a fine day.

Cooking outdoors reminded me of a picnic long ago, when I was five and bare-chested and my parents hadn't started fighting. We grilled hot dogs, drank Cokes in bottles, ate potato chips and bologna sandwiches outdoors. Everything tasted so good. Only my memory wasn't in color and I couldn't remember the day itself. I only remembered the black and white photograph with worn edges, that I touched so many times.

I wondered what kind of eggs Frank would like if he came back and how many to make and who would end up eating. If Frank wasn't back by the time they were done, I would invite the strange girl. I wanted to know her. We were related, after all, through the man we loved.

I cracked the eggs, one at a time, marveling at how orange their yolks were. What a difference between country chickens that live freely, eating whatever they pick off the ground, and mass-produced hens.

There are places where hundreds of chickens live locked up in long barns, each alone in its own little stall, under glaring lights, kept constantly on, forcing the hens to lay eggs around the clock. No rest for those chickens. No exercise either. They don't even grow feathers. And I had the nerve to bitch about how I was brought up.

Sunny side up, I decided, and my eggs sizzled healthily in the frying pan. I tossed the shells and poked at the whites, to see if they were done. I wasn't the least bit hungry.

As I scooped the last egg up onto the plate, I heard a fierce noise. A series of sharp barks, one after another. Even though I'd never heard one, I knew instantly it was a machine gun. It sounded like it came from the pond.

Several minutes after it stopped, I got the nerve to check it out. Approaching the area slowly, I noticed tiny pieces of wood scattered all over the ground. A small section from the neck of Frank's guitar hung on a low branch of a tree, the steel string still dangling from it. The remainder of Frank's most prized possession was in a thousand pieces, floating in the murky green water.

Frank was crouched on the bank, his eyes buried in his hands, as if he could make the whole scene disappear.

When he finally looked up, he took a deep breath and let out a huge sigh. His eyes scanned the dark hills around us. His face was more vulnerable than I had ever known it.

"There are guerrillas in these mountains," he said. His voice shook when he spoke.

"Gorillas?"

I realized as I said it that gorillas couldn't possibly be what he was talking about. This wasn't Africa. I tried to cover my mistake. "There's an elephant out there, too," I said. The laugh between my words rang false. Neither of us was in a very funny mood.

"Those guys think they're so lawless. They'll have to get a lot more, before anyone pays attention," Frank said. He pretended to shrug off his fear. "They're probably just drug dealers. Who cares?"

I'd always thought revolution was called for and that Latin revolutionaries were particularly sexy. But when I pictured a bunch right behind the next tree, it wasn't romantic at all.

"Is that who shot your guitar?" I asked.

"No. But it was probably one of his guns." Frank picked up a piece of wood off the ground and tossed it into the pond.

"Did Eva do it?" I asked.

Frank didn't answer.

I thought I felt someone behind me, but no one was there.

"It's not safe here," I said. "Is it?"

"You think it's safe anywhere?" he snapped.

Tree roots stuck up in the ground beneath me and made it hard for me to get comfortable.

"Sure, lots of places," I said. The scar across Frank's chest shone purple in the sunset. I reached over to button his shirt for him. "Where did you get the scar?"

"Broken bottle." Frank held his lips tight, like a small boy trying to pretend the bloody cut didn't really hurt. "It was my fault. He's dead, anyway."

The scar felt thick and bumpy as I ran my fingers gently over it.

"Stop it!" Frank hissed between gritted teeth, yanking my hand away.

He suddenly grabbed me by both shoulders so tightly it hurt. "Look at me, Sean," he yelled. "I-don't-want-this! I have nothing to give you. Do you hear? Nothing."

It was just like my fantasy, the way he grabbed me. Only it didn't feel good.

"*Nothing*, damn it, can't you hear me?" He dug his fingernails into my arms, shaking me wildly, spitting as he screamed, "Do you hear me? I don't want this!"

I stared at him, terrified.

When he let go, the inside of my arm burned. Tiny drops of blood surfaced on the half-moon wounds.

I searched Frank's face for the guy who had once made love to me.

"The eclipse is in the morning," I whispered. "Maybe...."

"Why did you even come here, Sean? I told you it would be awful."

I looked to see if he really meant it. His eyes were cold as mirrors.

I took a deep breath and brushed myself off. There was no point in feeling hurt or angry.

Watching the eclipse alone would be worse than lonely. Maybe Frank would snap out of it. I walked slowly toward the house, picking the dangling bits of skin off the fingernail marks on my arm. I bit my lip to hold back angry tears.

As I approached, I saw a shadow move in the doorway. It was Eva leaning against the open door. She held a machine gun, upright, between her legs and she was gently stroking it.

Eva saw me and started humming an odd aggressive drone. I wanted to run back to Frank. But I knew there was no safety in Frank's arms.

I tried to smile and I kept my eye on the gun, its bayonet pointing at her chin. In my gentlest voice, I suggested she hand the gun to me. "I don't think you want that thing pointing up at your face. I'll set it down for you."

Eva obediently lifted the gun and handed it to me horizontally, like a sacred offering. I took it, leaving her open palms suspended in air. The empty hands of a starving child.

As if she had no strength on her own, Eva's legs buckled under and she folded onto the ground. I knelt to set the gun down. Eva curled into a fetal position. I scooped her up onto my lap and put my arms around her. Her warm breath was moist on my neck. A single tear glistened in the moonlight as it rolled down her cheek.

I found a soft place in the dirt and leaned against the side of the house. Eva nuzzled up to me and sobbed. I wondered if she had purposely shot the guitar, jealous as I was, because he always held it so close. Or did she aim at Frank and miss?

I stroked her hair and told her everything was okay. Her tears kept coming, slow and steady as the trickling stream of a forgotten faucet.

Ana comes to me, in the warmest of dreams, her long pink hair, soft and sweet as cotton candy. She takes me to a place where everyone sings, and shows me how to be a lady in a long white dress, eating delicate flowers at a table full of children saying grace.

She strokes my head as I lay in white panties on cool white sheets and we listen to a song from the damp red earth. It is an ancient ballad, in the voice Frank always listened for. I hear the words and realize they are mine.

It is the prayer I held inside so long, the cry that aims for distant ears, the wish so primitive and deep, it was engraved in the pottery of the ancients, who recognized it as The One Fierce Desire – impossible to humanly fulfill.

A breeze woke me, whistling through the trees. Eva still slept in my arms.

Beside us, between the leaves of a bush, a thousand tiny crescent moons danced in the dazzling twilight. My desire to look up at the sun was almost irresistible. I didn't feel afraid. I felt respectful, a brand new feeling, small, but worthy of its self.

The wind grew louder. The sky darkened. Crisp shadows moved slowly in the dust. Covering her head with my own shadow, I carried Eva inside and lay her down on Frank's empty bed. Her face looked so very tranquil, beyond good dreams to no dreams at all.

I wondered if she would ever recover from loving Frank. For now, her mouth hung open in a silent call of surrender, like she had been crying for years and someone had finally heard.

Shimmering shadows covered the ground, and the trees were vibrant. I wanted to look up, but I knew it wasn't safe until the sun was totally blocked. Dozens of birds suddenly took flight from the trees, stirring the swirling breeze.

Then everything went silent. Even the birds stopped singing. The sky was dark, and I was surrounded by sparkling stars. A warm rush of calm spread through my body.

I looked up to see a bright red circle surround the sun. And the most magnificent radiance I have ever experienced. Pure pearly white light. A sight so truly wondrous, it seemed to answer all questions and meet all needs.

I closed my eyes the moment I saw the sun's diamond ring, and turned my head quickly, so I would not be blinded. The pure red round image paused briefly on my eyelids, a kiss from God's lips.

A symphony of trumpets seemed to come from the horizon. I felt the rumble of an earthquake and was more curious than frightened. But when the trumpet played again, I recognized the call of elephantine pleasure.

The Mayans knew exactly what the stars would do, when the sun would pass behind the moon. They also knew that coincidence was Motherfather's way of remaining anonymous.

I heard my elephant friend splashing and braying as I ran to the pond. I couldn't help but scream with delight.

Motherfather. How fucking brilliant.

Enrique emerged from his bath and shook himself off. I could feel the spray from twenty feet away.

When Enrique saw me, he stopped, scrutinized my face and

walked toward me. As he got close, he stopped again and turned around a few times. He reached his trunk and explored my body. Then he started flapping his ears and braying with pleasure.

He looked a little thin and worse for the wear. There were holes in one ear, probably from people shooting at him. But the instant I saw the wrinkles around his sweet sad eyes, I knew that he never really killed anyone. If he even came close, it was because he was threatened and panicked. There might be such a thing as a simply mean elephant, but I never knew one.

The gun still lay in the dirt. I wasn't sure if it was loaded, but I didn't want to leave it with Frank and Eva. So I took it inside, laid it in the bottom of my duffel bag and tossed my clothes in over it. I zipped up the bag and threw it over my shoulder, making sure the gun pointed up toward the heavens, where bullets can't harm a soul.

I tapped Enrique on the leg and he knelt down. Using his knee as a step, I hoisted myself onto his back and scooted up to his thick neck. I tucked my legs under his huge ears and felt immensely comfortable. Riding Enrique was one thing I knew how to do. Perhaps we would ride all the way to Venice Beach and watch the ocean. Or I'd take him to my mother's house so I could say I'm sorry. With a beast of Enrique's stature by my side, no one would ever mess with me again. We'd never run out of gas.

Or maybe I'd find a better home for Enrique, and a better home for me. Anything was possible. I knew I could imagine a whole new life for myself. Years of miracles were in store.

Frank emerged from the night house as we passed. He took off his goggles and squinted up at us, like he could not believe what he saw. Perhaps he was imagining it. Maybe we both were.

"Did you see it?" he asked, his eyebrows raised. "Do you see that?" He turned around in circles. We were still surrounded by all the colors of dawn, a three hundred and sixty degree twilight.

"Yes." The view from Enrique was spectacular. "Yes!"

Frank shook his head back and forth and started laughing like the beauty was all too much for him. I'd never heard him laugh like that, and part of me wanted so badly to laugh with him. But it was far too late to laugh with Frank. I wanted love that was worth something.

I turned Enrique toward the gate. "Good-bye Frank," I said, in a stage whisper that almost strangled me. There were a lot of things I could have said, but Good-bye was the kindest.

"Yeah, right," he said. He must have been stunned by the magnificence of the eclipse, because his "Yeah, right" was rather reverent.

"Vaya con Dios." I smiled, knowing that I would.

I couldn't tell why he looked so shocked, whether it was just because I was leaving or because I was leaving on the back of an elephant, in the afterglow of the eclipse.

I couldn't help but milk the moment of my exit. I raised my arms to the sky, like "Look Ma! No hands!"

Frank didn't even notice. He had pulled a note pad out of his pocket and was writing. But that was okay with me. We both needed something bigger and more ancient than romance.

In the pond I could see the reflection of the crescent moon. The sun was back. The hole in my soul felt warm as a hearth fire.

Acknowledgments

My thanks to the those people who have offered valuable suggestions and/or support: Jim and Pam Smothers, Chuck and Ava Fries, Jim Krusoe, Jamie Robin, Francine Prose and the Sewanee Writers' Conference, Susan Hayden, Susan Traylor, Judith Searle, Francesca Lia Block, Javier Aki, Dawna Kemper, Lou Beach and Ron Meckler.

www.ingramcontent.com/pod-product-compliance
Lightning Source LLC
Chambersburg PA
CBHW031202260626
47169CB00004B/1220